BAM! THAD EELS

SYBIL DARLETTE

Library of Congress Control Number 2014919830
ISBN 978-0-972-3042-9-0

Manufactured in Phoenix, Arizona, United States of America

thadeels.weebly.com

Acknowledgements

Dedicated to the handful of family members, friends, parents of friends, ex-co-workers and several others who made this book possible. Cover Design by SelfPubBookCovers.com/Asha

CHAPTER ONE

The Mix

"Aint no relief for a single mama", Glammer murmured as she rolled out of bed. With eyes partially opened, she stood, unsteadily, on her tip toes desperately reaching towards the ceiling as she leaned backwards taking in the air of a fresh new day. She had been on her own since the birth of her son Jontavious. After constant bickering with her mother about the upbringing of the child, Glammer packed her bags and moved in with her best friend Anna Rosa. At sixteen years old, Glammer became another client for Welfare. Her name, for housing assistance, was at the bottom of the list. At Anna Rosa's, Glammer earned her keep by caring for Jontavious as well as Anna Rosa's two sets of twins. Reko and Meko were nearly two years old and had been born before Anna Rosa moved to the U.S. to be with her husband Javier. After six months of marriage, Javier divorced her for a nightclub stripper and literally disappeared. A few weeks later, she got a part-time job, as a housekeeper at a run down motel across town where she meet Darvell.

Together, they produced Ja'lil and Shaquille who were now nearly eight months old. On weekends, there was never a quiet morning. If Anna Rosa wasn't fighting with Darvell, the older twins were running through the house throwing toys and screaming to go outside, while the younger twins cried out to be changed or fed. Everything was up to Glammer until Anna Rosa gave up her fight with Darvell and called the police to have him escorted off the property. Glammer sat by the phone, holding Jontavious, reminiscing about the day she meet Johnny. *It was the start of a new school year. She was in the tenth grade and home room was about over when Johnny walked in and gave the teacher some paperwork. Everyone starred at him in awe because of his size. Johnny looked like a college student as he strolled in, dressed casually, in a pair of sagging camouflaged knee length shorts, exposing the teal green band of his blue underwear. He was wearing a tan muscle shirt that did him justice. Standing at least six foot three, he had the new growth of a beard that had been shaved just days ago, and he smelled of expensive designer cologne. "Watch the Marx", he said , as he passed by some of the other boys. All the girls got dreamy eyed just watching him walk over to his desk.* Johnny was 20 and had been held back several times for missing too many school days and not making them up during the summer. State law was graduate by 21 or go to adult school. He had a little under six months to be there.

Glammer wanted more than anything for him to call and request to see her and Jontavious. She knew that if Johnny called, she could get away for a while. He'd take them to a cheap motel where they'd spend the day playing house, watching movies and eating fast food. They'd spend the night there and if she played her cards right, when he dropped her off, he'd give her at least forty dollars. She really could use the money. Two weeks was a long time to wait for that next Welfare check and food voucher. How she wished Johnny would call.

An hour later police cars arrived with blue lights flashing. They stormed right into Anna Rosa's house, went straight to the bedroom and hauled Darvell out in handcuffs, while his twin boys watched. The phone finally rang and it was Johnny. Glammer could hardly hear him due to the inside noise. Anna Rosa was standing inside the screen door yelling profanities in Spanish while waving her middle finger at Darvell who was being thrown into the backseat of a police car by the back of his jeans. Suddenly, one by one, all the babies began to cry, including Jontavious, who was just about sound asleep.

Glammer yelled to Anna Rosa to watch the babies while she ran to the back room to talk with Johnny. He wanted to see them, but he couldn't. He had been arrested for "possession with intent". He wanted Glammer to sale her food card and use her voucher to bail him out of jail. He told her how much he loved her and Jontavious and convinced her that he wanted them to be a real family. He even asked her to marry him. Two weeks later Glammer bailed him out of jail. They had lunch at Johnny's mother's house, while she played happily with her grandson. Later, Johnny barrowed his mother's car and drove Glammer and Jontavious back to Anna Rosa's. He kissed them, gave Glammer twenty dollars, and drove off. She never heard from him again.

Anna Rosa was a half block from her home. It was mid-summer and she was starting to regret cutting her long hair. The heat of the day felt like smoldering hot coals on the back of her naturally tanned neck. Each step felt like twelve leaps as she rushed excitedly down the sidewalk fanning her face with a sweat stained bus schedule. She had some really good news for Glammer who had been desperately seeking employment for the past few weeks. Anna Rosa would finally see that sparkle of ambition she saw in her friend's eyes the first night they met.

It was Anna Rosa's third month as a housekeeper at the Nitecap Motel. She was just finishing up room 127, "The Paradise in Ecstasy" Honey-

moon Suite. It was the most popular and expensive room in the entire motel. It featured a separate living area with regular beige carpeting and all
the comforts of home. Behind the scenic mural divider wall, sunken in the
floor, was a gorgeous sparkly red heart-shaped jacuzzi, with a lovely golden
swan neck faucet. Once filled with water, the jacuzzi would slowly rotate
to the extended versions of various love songs. This area of the room had
red shag carpeting, as if it had been ripped right out of the seventies . To
compliment the setting even more, about 12 feet to the right of the jacuzzi
was a high, heart shaped automated bed that had two steps leading up to
it. In the center of the headboard was a painting of Cupid with his arrow
pointing to an attached coin slot. By inserting four quarters, the bed would
vibrate continuously for one hour.

Above the bed was a huge fake glass mirror with a built in clap acti-
vated dimmer light. Anna Rosa was putting new bars of soap in the vanity
area when Glammer walked in carrying her newborn son. Almost walking
into them, darting from around the corner, Anna Rosa couldn't get an
apologetic word out before she saw Johnny walking in carrying a diaper
bag and portable baby swing.

"I'll get the other bags", he roared to Glammer, dropping the items on
the floor halfway into the room as he turned lazily and strolled back to the
car.

Overcome by the deepness of his voice, Anna Rosa dashed back into the
vanity area secretly scanning Johnny from head to toe as if he was some
kind of chocolate covered tropical eye candy.

"Damn Girlfriend! Where you find that!?", she asked Glammer, approvingly. She grabbed a tissue from her cart and dapped her forehead for sweat
beads, she questioned, "Thatcho baby daddy?!".

Before Glammer could respond, Anna Rosa continued excitedly, "Girl, I
got some stuff you can use." Wondering what she could possibly mean,
Glammer put Jontavious on the bed and followed Anna Rosa who was

waving her over, while pulling, what looked like, groceries from beneath a blanket under her cleaning cart. " I found this bottle of champagne this morning in room 207. They must've forgot they had it. New too! Un-opened. It was going home with me for

my party next weekend, but I hate to see a good night and a good man wasted", Anna Rosa said, smiling at Glammer, as she darted out into the hallway, and back in, checking for walk-bys. "Here", she directed, giving Glammer an extra box of bubble bath and bath salt. "So, whatcho name girlfriend?', she asked,' cause I got something here I'd only give a friend and everybody could use a friend". "Hey, you wanna come to my party next weekend?', Anna Rosa asked while pulling an invitation out of her pocket, 'If you do, I'll give you the good stuff. It'll have that man of yours thinking he's king of the city. Don't worry about a baby-sitter for my party, I got four boy,. two sets of twins. Call me a day in advance and I'll know to get an-other sitter."

"A party?', Glammer asked, 'yeah, sure I'll come", she added.

Knowing that she had somewhat gained Glammer's trust, Anna Rosa pulled out a pound of strawberries and a can of chocolate sauce. "Here you go', she said, 'see you at the party." She had just pulled her cart out of the room when Johnny returned with the overnight bags. Repositioning the blanket on the bottom of the cart Anna Rosa moved over to the next room and knocked loudly on the door. "Housekeeping!".

The following Saturday, Glammer attended Anna Rosa's party. It turned out to be a bachlorette party for her cousin Rosita. Glammer quickly learned that she was the youngest one actually attending the celebration. There appeared to be people

her age upstairs, but she soon found out that they were babysitters and not allowed downstairs during the party. The gathering was a success. It was totally complete with male dancers prancing around in G-strings, gy-rating to the beat of the music. There were tacos, pizza, barbecue, cake, tequila, champagne, and lots of cigarette smoke. Glammer witnessed one lady faint when a dancer strutted over to her and brushed a strain of hair out of her face. Glammer remained quiet throughout most of the party. She was learning a lot about everything by listening to the others. Everyone seemed to be between nineteen and twenty-one years old. The majority of them had at least three children. She continued to listen closely as she learned a lot about babies, boys, men, and the welfare system. "Finding out you're pregnant ain't no big thing these days, just 'mo money and 'mo benefits", one tall skinny lady in a hooker wig said through a mouth full of pizza.

"I know dat's right!', the girl behind her announced, 'and if you just think you pregnant, they got that pill you take the next morning. What ya'll thank 'bout that?" Another hooker looking lady replied, "That new pill, shoot! That's another hundred or two a month just for one more baby! Who'd turn that down? It ain't like you gotta promise to go back to school or learn a trade or something. You just have to work 2-3 days a week, something part-time and they hand out the benefits. Now I ain't always for hand outs, but I aint ever gonna be rich and free is free!"

"It sure wasn't like this in Mexico', Anna Rosa said, 'it was hard. As long as people has been wanting to come to the United States, it's all for the same reason; so that things will be a little easier." For the first time Glammer spoke up after hearing what Anna Rosa had to say. "Don't you wish you were rich, or at least not on Welfare?,' she asked,' Don't you want something better?". The chubby lady replied. "Why? I get to sleep all day, watch the soaps, do what I want and my mama ain't taking cure of me!"

"Who you anyway?, 'she asked Glammer,' I though the teens were up-stairs baby-sitting." Feeling the tension boil, Anna Rosa jumped in, "This is Glammer, one of my friends from work. I invited her."

"Glammer"., the chubby lady said. "How many babies do you have Ms. Glammer?", she asked sarcastically.

"I have one", Glammer replied.

"Um-hmm", the hooker- looking lady said, while rocking her head side to side. "I should've known', she added, 'still wet behind the ears. (she paused) I can smell the milk on your breath from way over here. 'Mo babies, 'mo money, mo benefits. Sometimes, if you're lucky, you get a house out ud. Work when you want and pay fifty dollars a month rent. But you don't know nothing 'bout that", she said while passing out from intoxication.

Anna Rosa held Glammer's hand in support, " Don't worry,' she whispered,'

Sizzle not my friend. She's a friend of Rosita's sister. She always needin' something'. Look at her, she needin' some teeth." She bumped Glammer on the arm and smiled.

By the time Anna Rosa arrived home from the bus stop, her white Nitecap Motel tee-shirt was drenched with sweat and plastered to her upper torso revealing a very uncomfortable beige bra.

Glammer was in the kitchen, giving out snacks, when Anna Rosa appeared smiling widely.

"You like money right?', she asked Glammer. picking up the younger set of twins simultaneously, coz you just been hired! Hosea said I could bring anyone to work with me tomorrow and if she do good, he'll keep her. We gon work togetha. Yay!", she said in excitement.

Glammer was so excited that she could hardly stand still. She starting pacing hastily back and forth. "Oh, well, I , I guess I'll have to call mama and see if she can keep Jontavious. I don't know Anna Rosa, you'll need a new baby-sitter. It's just so sudden, I don't know what to do!", she yelled while starting to sweat profusely with worry.

"Okay, so check this out', Anna Rosa said, calming her down,' I called my cousin Rosita, you remember her right, from the party? Anyway, she not working right now and she say, she can watch our boys." She put the boys back onto the play mat.

Slapping herself in the chest with her hand she continued, "You will be working in housekeeping with me. I'm yo trainer! All you have to do is what I tell you to do and everything will be fine. So, what you say?', she asked, 'you wit me?"

Taking a deep breath, Glammer paused and answered, " I guess I got me a job."

Anna Rosa thought briefly about her first husband and the fact that he was behind on child support.

"That's right girl', Anna Rosa said happily, 'gotta make some money. Can't always depend on baby daddy."

Darvell was sobering up, and it was getting cloudy. He decided to crank up the old BMW and drive Anna Rosa and Glammer to work. He figured it would be a treat for them because they wouldn't have to stand at the bus stop in the rain. It would also give him a chance to talk Anna Rosa out of some extra money to feed his daily habit. He'd lost his job at the liquor store for stealing twelve cases of malt liquor, at closing time last week, when he thought he had disabled the security camera by cutting the wires. In reality, he'd cut the wires to the old dummy camera and was caught on tape under the very watchful eyes of several very small discreet cameras placed in various areas of the store. To keep Anna Rosa from finding out, he requested all small bills when he cashed his final paycheck. That way, his wallet would still look thick if she just happen to see it. Unfortunately, when you have a habit, two hundred, fifty-seven dollars and twenty eight cents can go fast, even when you're still living home with your mother. His only problem was mama wasn't trying to give an allowance to a grown man with two kids, even if he did say that his boss fired him for buying too much liquor and suspected that he was intoxicated. Nonetheless, he was down to his last fifty dollars and he wanted a little more to get him through the week until his unemployment check arrived. He'd planned on getting it from Anna Rosa, but he had to be careful how he got it. He didn't want to end up spending the weekend in jail over another episode of "baby mama" drama.

Nearly driving through a stop light, Darvell slammed on the brakes after hearing the girls scream. " What's wrong wit ya'll?", he asked nonchalantly.

Glammer kept quiet. Anna Rosa responded with a hard stare and sigh.

While preparing to get some money from Anna Rosa, Darvell turned the radio's volume down, sparing other drivers the horrible sound of loud bass beats escaping busted speakers, partially repaired with gray tape.

"Yeah!, dat da shit thure." He said, while holding a skinny brown cigar out the corner of his mouth and pointing at the radio displaying a huge, fake gold nugget ring. "Dem boys cole!", he said.

The light changed to green and Darvell jetted through it driving another half mile before turning into the driveway of the Nitecap motel. When the car stopped, he unlocked the doors just long enough for Glammer to open her door. Then he locked them, keeping Anna Rosa in the car as Glammer walked towards the motel entrance for her first day on the job. "Stop play'n Darvell, you gonna make me late for work", Anna Rosa told him.

"What?', he asked, smiling coyly, ' oh, so now yo mane caint have no sugga or nothing'. It's like that today, huh?", Darvell asked, trying to charm her. He tried to put his arm around her neck. "It's okay', he said, 'daddy understand. You must be on the rag today, that's fine".

Ignoring his last comment, Anna Rosa leaned over and gave Darvell a peck on the lips, trying to avoid the smoking cigar still dangling from his mouth. Quickly, she unlocked the car door, got out and started walking away.

"Hole up!, hole up!", Darvell called out to her, while rushing out of the car trying not to trip over his sagging designer jeans. "Com mere a minute", he told her. Anna Rosa checked her watch and saw that she had five minutes to clock in for work. "Com mere girl. Damn!', Darvell called out, grabbing his crotch with one hand and waving her over with the other. 'Got me falling all outta my pansies and shit." Realizing the only way for her to leave the parking lot without Darvell trying to follow her inside the motel was to go see what the idiot wanted. "What now Darvell', Anna Rosa asked,' I told you I have to clock in."

Finally removing the cigar from his dried lips and flickering it onto the pavement to burn out, he pulled Anna Rosa into an insincere embrace, lowered his voice and said, " I need to hold 'bout twenty dollars baby, gotta take care of sumpt'n. "Whatchu gotta take care of Darvell.' she asked. ' Can't you use YOUR money?,' I thought you say you still work at that liquor store." She pulled away from him.

"Don't worry about my bitness." Darvell told her. "Omma mane, I takes care of mine." he said.

"Then why don't you take care of your babies then. You can't do that if you gotta get money from the mama all the time Darvell!", she yelled angrily. "Stop playne now. Com mo", he told her, pretending to care about her feelings.

"What you need it fo anyway?', he asked. 'You s'pose to be hure workin' all day."

Anna Rosa angrily stepped away from him, arguing in Spanish as she reached into her pocket pulled out a twenty dollar bill and threw it at Darvell as she hurried towards the motel entrance.

Darvell picked the money up from the ground. "What? What you say? Speak English bitch!", he told her as he tucked the money into his pocket. "Yeah, yeah, aw'ight', he added, not comprehending a single word, 'see if I pick yo ass up this evening." He jumped back into the car and peeled out of the driveway nearly crashing into oncoming traffic as he drove away. The car swerved out of control and backfired loudly as he left.

Anna Rosa made it to the time clock, punched in at eight o'clock, and rushed off to the restroom to splash some cold water on her face in an attempt to calm down before starting her work day. Glammer emerged from one of the stalls and saw her standing in front of the mirror patting her face dry.

"You okay?", Glammer asked her.

"Yeah', Anna Rosa replied, 'we may have to take the bus home today."

"Okay". Glammer said.

Anna Rosa and Glammer entered room 101 at the motel. Step by step, Anna Rosa explained what needed to be done and the correct way to do it, then she carefully explained the importance of wearing rubber gloves. Most importantly, she told Glammer to make sure and clean between the nightstand and the bed. Always place the remote control on the nightstand in front of the telephone and never, ever touch anything containing body fluids with your bare hands.

She pointed out that glass and windows are to be cleaned with a mixture of hot water and vinegar, use bleach and hot water on the bathroom floor. always empty the trash cans in rooms with double beds, only change the bed that was used, but if the pillows are moved, change the pillow cases. Always spray two squirts of room deodorizer in the air before leaving the room. and double check it before marking it off your list and reporting it as clean and vacant. Everything is to be done the same way in all rooms.

Just before Anna Rosa left Glammer to work on her own, she showed her how to stock her housekeeping cart from top to bottom, gave her a quick hug, and told her to go to the laundry room, at noon, for lunch.

Glammer began her job as instructed by her trusted friend Anna Rosa. She changed the linens, emptied trash, scrubbed the toilet, mopped the floor and cleaned the mirrors. Knowing that she had more than one room to clean, Glammer worked at top speed, finishing in thirty minutes. Realizing that she had worked up a sweat,

Glammer decided to take a quick break, and breathe a little, before squirting deodorizer in the air. Forgetting that she left the room's door open, she found herself daydreaming of being on vacation and sitting in her own motel room. "Cuze me maam', a somewhat deep whinny voice called out, from the door way, startling her, 'I'm staying over for another night, can I get some clean towels?" Startled, Glammer leaped to her feet and darted towards the open door.

"Yeah, sure', she told the short, frail guy standing there, 'here you are,' she replied, giving the little man a fresh set of towels.

"Thank you maam", he said, as he pranced down the walkway in his yellow and baby blue silk lounge set. With his long, wet, stringy blond hair, air drying in the wind, he made it apparent that he'd come out of the closet years ago. After staring for a second in disbelief, Glammer got the deodorizer from the cart, squirted it twice in the air and vacated the room, quickly closing the door behind her. Marking the first room off her list, she was ready to report it as clean and vacant.

"Housekeeping!", Glammer called out, knocking loudly on the door.

"They gone, child", a fat old lady peeping out from the room across the hall told her. "You dat new girl Anna Rose brought in?", she asked suspiciously.

"Anna Rosa', Glammer said, correcting her,' yeah, she brought me in this morning."

"Anna Rose', the old lady repeated,' you can name somebody Anna and you can sniff a rose, but you caint name somebody Anna and sniff a Rosa", she explained as she spat brown liquid into a white foam cup.

Wiping her mouth, she wobbled across the walkway and extended a damp hand, "Clara Matty', she said, 'folks call me Mrs. Matty".

"I'm Glammer", Glammer told her.

Smelling like a mixture of mint muscle rub and stale tobacco, she stepped a little closer.

"Okay Glammer', Mrs. Matty said, 'when you finish with dat there room, come over here and knock on my dough and we'll walk up to the laundry room for lunch. See what yo' friend Anna Rose up to. You know I saw her this morning with that no good mane of hers. She need to stay away from him. (she paused) You know, he told her to get rid of them twins when she was pregnut. Um-hmm, hud wit my own two yels. You come get Mrs. Matty now. (she nodded) I be here." Finally, she shut her mouth and went back into her darkened room.

Mrs. Matty was in her early 60's and had been working at the motel since it opened ten years ago. Some folk who frequent the motel on a regular basis said that Mrs. Matty was here when it was shut down back in the 60's.

Across the hall, Glammer was having a major problem cleaning the room. As soon as she opened the door, she was hit in the face, by a burst of heavy pungent smoke rushing in her direction to escape the room. Covering her nose and mouth with a clean washcloth, Glammer ran to the window and opened it as wide as possible. She stuck he head out and breathed for a while before turning around to inspect the room. On one bed, there were six large pizza boxes piled up with a bottle of opened salad dressing oozing out onto the comforter. Surrounding the second bed were several fast food bags filled with trash and half-eaten food. In the ashtray, on top of the nightstand, there were several little white hand rolled cigarettes with brownish-green oregano looking stuff coming out into the ashtray. On the floor, between the two double beds, were two used condoms still containing body fluids.

Almost in a state of shock from the filthiness of the room, Glammer entered the bathroom and saw three syringes atop the vanity, and thick urine splashes on and around the toilet. Feeling almost embarrassed, she went to her cart, put on two pairs of rubber gloves and proceeded to clean the room.

While getting a contact high from the smoke still lingering in the room, Glammer made a promise to herself that she would not end up like Mrs. Matty. She would not get stuck in a rut where the only job she qualified for was housekeeping. She owed something better to herself, and her son. Besides that, she wanted her mother to be proud of her again.

"This is only temporary', she said, as she dumped the ashtray, 'only temporary". "The laundry room was tucked away around back of the motel. Although the room itself was air conditioned, the heavy duty dryers made the temperature increase another twenty degrees. Walking nearly around the entire building looking for the laundry room, Glammer finally walked in. All the housekeepers, including Mrs. Matty, who wasn't working that day, were sitting at a long table about to eat lunch. Glammer hesitated joining the crowd because she forgot that Mrs. Matty wanted to walk to the laundry room with her and she didn't knock on the old lady's door. It didn't matter anyway, Mrs. Matty was already in there. Anna Rosa stood up surveying the room, making sure all the housekeepers for present before clocking out for lunch. When she saw Glammer standing over by the old pay phone, she waved her over.

"Hey girlfriend', how you com'n with those rooms?"

"That's Glammer there', Mrs Matty told one of the ladies, 'I met her this morning. Um-hmm, she can clean a room in about thirty minutes. She good, Hosea gonna keep her", she said through a mouth full of food. Glammer walked over to Anna Rosa who was handing her an ice cold soda.

"This is Glammer ladies', Anna Rosa announced, 'she is going to be working with us for a while." Glammer smiled and spoke to the group before occupying the empty seat next to Anna Rosa. As soon as she got comfortable, the hair on the back of her neck stood up. "Don't you look familiar?", an intimidating voice said from behind her. Glammer turned around and saw the skinny, hooker looking lady from the bachlorette party.

Oh joy, she thought. Forcing a cheerful smile, she spoke.

"Hey, how you doing?", she asked.

"I do fine 'lil girl', she answered, 'I do fine every day!'

"Leave her 'lone Spicey', Mrs. Matty said,' it's lunchtime, shouldn't you be outside making some extra money?" Mrs. Matty winked at Spicey. "You know, some special money?"

Puffing on a cigarette and exhaling towards the ceiling, spicey responded, "Mine ya bitness, heffer." Spicey pulled a tiny bottle of perfume out of her cleavage, dabbed some behind each ear, glared at Glammer and walked out.

"Ooooh child, you aint gonna let that Spicey work with Glammer awya?", Mrs. Matty asked.

Anna Rosa, who was busy going over paperwork with Glammer totally ignored her so she instantly started talking to Stacy, the other new girl, who started a day before Glammer.

"Spicey aint nothing but a 'ho. (*she paused*) I saw her yestaday getting in a van wit some white mane. He drove 'ran back. She stayed in there about an hour. Van justa rockin', Um-hmm, (*she nodded*) 'ho'n."

She turned towards Glammer, who was still discussing issues with Anna Rosa. Stuffing a tiny sausage and a cracker in her mouth, she said to Glammer, "Here baby, you want these chips? Ain gonna eat all dis salt. Mrs. Matty gotta watch her pressure."

The lunch timer dinged and everyone got up and returned to work, except Mrs. Matty, she went back to her darkened room to sit in the chair by the window.

Glammer was pushing her cart outside when the A-Tek Vending truck arrived. The new driver had no idea where the vending machines were located, or who he should get to sign the paperwork. He saw Glammer in a housekeeping smock walking down the sidewalk. After watching her for a while, he parked close to the sidewalk, he jumped out of the truck and approached Glammer.

"Excuse me Mrs. Lady", he said. Glammer turned around and picked her mouth up off the ground when she saw him. He had on a olive green uniform short set, complete with the little baseball style cap. Pretending to be busy, she tried to keep from staring.

"Whom do I get to accept this order and sign my paperwork", he asked her.

"Just take it up there to the lobby, they'll sign it for you", she replied still checking out his biceps. Knowing that he had made quite an impression, he done some quick thinking.

"I own my own company. Here's one of my cards. If you ever need some snacks, or want another job, give me a call.", he lied.

Taking the card, Glammer quickly examined it.

"A-Tek is your company?", she asked surprisingly. He flashed her a quick smile displaying pearly white teeth. He had all his front teeth and not a single one was gold! "Well, actually, it's my granddad's company', he told her, ' I figured you wouldn't go out with me unless I said it was my company." He leaned down and read her name tag. He got so close that she could smell his expensive cologne.

"Glammer, that's pretty", he said.

"What's your name, A-Tek?', she asked.

He smiled and leaned against the truck. "I'm Enrique. Enrique Tekzonni", he replied. Glammer looked at his business card again.

"A-Tek. So who is A again", she asked.

"A is Alex Tekzonni, my granddad. If you let me call you tonight, I'll give you my complete family history", he promised.

That night Enrique and Glammer spent hours talking on the phone before he persauded her to go for a drive with him. When he arrived, Glammer was wowed by his 2014 shinny new sports utility vehicle. She rushed to the door to greet him as he stepped out of the fancy SUV.

"I hope I didn't overdue it', he said,' I was going to bring out the convertible, but I thought it might get a little to hot if we decide to park and stare at the stars."

"Oh the truck's fine", she managed to say, holding out a welcoming hand.

"I have someone for you to meet", she warned.

"Is it a parent or an old mean grandmother", he joked.

"Neither', Glammer, told him, picking up her toddler,' this is my son ,Jontavious."

Enrique smiled and reached out to hold the baby. Noticing the little boys smile, he stated, "Friendly little guy, isn't he?", he asked Glammer.

Glammer was still waiting for him to ask if there were other children. A question she'd gotten used to. Instead, he kneeled down in the floor and started tickling and wrestling with the baby. "Oh, you're gonna be a jock someday aren't ya fellow", he asked Jontavious who gooed and cooed happily as they played.

Still amazed at the attention Enrique was giving Jontavious, Glammer stepped out the door for a better view of the shiny SUV parked in the driveway.

"Expecting someone?", he asked, noticing her peering outside.

Slightly embarrassed, Glammer stepped back inside the livingroom and closed the door. "Oh, no, ', she told him,' it's just that, well this is my friend's house."

"She didn't know I was coming over, huh?", he assumed, while standing up with the baby. "Ya know', he told her, 'lets go. I'm not an expert on babies, but the last time I baby sat, I discovered that they love long rides."

Trying not to look too excited about riding in a vehicle that appeared to be in perfect condition, she hesisitated.

"Well, taye taye usually takes his nap around this time", she responded.

"Oh come on', he pleaded,' the drive will put him to sleep. If you want, I'll put the tv on, in back, and he can watch cartoons until he falls asleep."

The man has a T.V. in that thing ! She thought. Glammer couldn't afford to refuse his request any longer, she didn't want to risk losing this guy. She took Jontavious away from Enrique. "If we're going for a drive, I guess he will need to put his shoes on", she told him.

"Oh, give them to me, I'll put them on him', Enrique requested,' I think he'll let me." Giving him the boy's shoes, Glammer walked towards the SUV and was about to open the front passenger side of the door when she heard Enrique call out to her. "Hey, don't you dare!"

Not knowing what he meant by the comment, Glammer backed away from the SUV and checked her hands, as if ink was all over them. After securing Jontavious in the build in car seat, Enrique walked around to where Glammer stood inspecting herself as if she had the plague.

"I'm a gentleman ma'lady', he charmed her, 'I'll get the door for you."

Never ever in her life having this kind of treatment from anyone, Glammer nearly fainted while trying to hide buckling knees, as he gently pulled her aside and opened the door. "This is how you treat a lady, son,' he called out to Jontavious, who was busy sucking on a pacifer and watching cartoons via satellite, 'remember this." he told him. When he put the SUV in gear and backed out the driveway, it didn't backfire and there was no smoke. In fact, if you didn't see for yourself, you wouldn't know you were moving at all. It was dusk, they drove until nightfall, then briefly parked alongside a deserted stretch of highway. "I can show you the stars here with binoculars, or we can drive to my apartment, and view them on the balcony with my telescope,' he suggested softly,' you'd get a much better view."

With curiosity growing larger by the minute, Glammer agreed that they should view the stars from the balcony of his apartment. Enrique drove a mile down the deserted highway and entered the ramp to the expressway leading away from familiar surroundings. With great concern, Glammer asked him timidly, "Where are we going?"

"To my apartment', he told her,' I thought you said it was okay?" Slowing down about to exit the expressway in case she changed her mind, he asked," You did say it was okay, right?"

Glammer hesitated," Yeah, but, where you live?', she asked, ' the next town over."

Smiling, he glanced at her, " I live in Trenton Hills", he informed.

Gasping, Glammer repeated, "Trenton Hills!"

"Yeah', Enrique replied,' is it too far for you? It's only a twenty minute drive this way." Glammer tried to regain her composure. "Oh, it's fine', she said,' I just didn't realize you lived out of the area", she told him.

Glammer knew all about Trenton Hills. It was a very affluent suburban area on the other side of the river. Getting there was similar to crossing the famous Brooklyn Bridge. It was so beautiful and she always wanted to live there. Growing up, her mother lost money, time and time again, on get rich quick schemes and working unthinkable overtime just to be able to afford an tiny efficiency apartment in Trenton Hills, only to find out, that they wouldn't let her get an efficiency apartment with a child. To make it even harder, she had to make four times the monthly rent within thirty days, for the length of her lease, to even qualify. That was BEFORE they said her credit wasn't good enough. Trenton Hills had the best of everything from parks to schools to entertainment centers. In Glammer's neighborhood, no one thought they could ever live in Trenton Hills. It was just that good. Enrique's apartment community was like vacationing at a colorful resort in the middle of nowhere. It was so peaceful and quiet. The grounds had the most beautiful green, Bermuda grass Glammer had ever seen. Lining the sidewalk leading to the property management office were little tiny colorful flowers.

There was even a lake with a gorgeous waterfall, built to resemble Niagara Falls. No matter what direction Glammer looked, she saw a pool. There were people out playing sand volleyball and washing their cars in the three bay carwash right there on the property! Everyone seemed to have their own double garage attached to their own apartment. The tennis courts had nets and was next to a building that said racquetball. In the back there appeared to be a child care facility, with playground equipment. It didn't have a single swing missing. Even on the basketball court, the baskets had nets! To Glammer, this was truly paradise and she wished with all her heart that she could live in Trenton Hills. Jontavious would have the best education allowed outside of private schools. It would be perfect. Enrique opened the garage door to reveal a burnt orange convertible sports car. "You have a roommate too?", Glammer asked.

"No, that's mine', he told her,' I was going to drive it, but changed my mind at the last minute." Glammer gulped. Wondering if it was all a dream.

"Three bedrooms and one lonely guy", he said.

"Why do you have three bedroom if it's just you", Glammer asked, still curious.

Closing the garage door he said calmly, " I like space."

CHAPTER TWO

Trenton Hills

Back in her darkened motel room, Mrs. Matty was listening to sancti-
fied gospel on the radio when her next door neighbor called to update
her on the progress of her house. "Yo house lookin' good Clara', Ms.
Lilly told her, 'the head mane say they gon put dat bay winda in tomorrow. You know the kind like Mawgie got down the street? Day almost done wit it."

"Oh child!, dat's good,' Mrs. Matty yelled into the phone,' dat show
good news ta me. Lawd ya!."

Mrs. Matty picked up a copy of some fake religious magazine and
started fanning with it. Rocking back and forth in a stationary chair,
expressing excitement, she reached over and got a container of snuff,
off the table, and stuffed a hunk of it inside her lower lip. "Om tied of
stayin' here', she told Lilly, 'walls closin' in on me. Dem young folk
runnin' 'ran while, and doin' all kinds of sin'n. You take dat girl we
tawk 'bout last week. Dat Glammer. She da smodd one. She don got

hussef a mane. A 'lil ole mixed boy!. Uh-hmm, tell me she don got hussef pregnutt too. (she paused) Show nuff."

Mrs. Matty reached over and got a foam cup off the nightstand and stuffed a tissue, from the pocket of her smock, into the bottom of the cup and spit a thick, cheek full of brown liquid into it. "Tell me he black and I-tel-yawn,' she informed,' his baby too. Po baby aint gon know what it is. Black, I-tel-yawn, black, heh!, heh! ,heh! (she paused to catch her breath) Oh lawdy mercy! Wew!', she picked up the foam cup and expectorated more brown liquid, 'uh-hmm. Now you take dat fun gal Anna Rose, she been needin' ta git ridda her mane. That Daw-vell, dey call em.", Mrs. Matty told Lillie.

Mrs. Matty heard a thump, then the sound of a car door shutting near her window. She leaned back to peep out the corner of the drapes, making sure she was well hidden in the darkness of her room.

"Look at him!, Look at him!', ahh chucks!, she said, 'you caint see him, heh, heh." Still peeping out the window, she continued her gossip.

"Dat dat Daw-vell. Uh, uh, Anna Rose mane. Lillie, you on dat Ah-bummafone, aintcha? You sound funny. Ah chucks now. Look at em. He out here eve'r other day wit dat white gal that u-sta work here. He must've seed Anna Rose work schedule cause when sheen here, he brings dat white gal and pay almost two hundred dollars for the honeymoon suite, buy'n chocolates and roses petals and thangs, while Anna Rose sitting up rockin' his babies. Heen try'n da do right bile. Dey git into it all da time here. He gon hit her one day. I know he is, Um-hmm. We gone hafta call da po-east. Watch'n see don't I tell ya 'bout it,", she said.

Knowing Spicey's family for years, Ms. Lille felt obligated to ask about her.

"Oh child, Spicey still 'ho'n. Tell me, she stayed in Trenton Hills all last week shakin' her tail at some fancy high society white boy poddy. She da only black face there and got all them rich mane folk pawing all ova. Dayne doin' nothin' but usin her. Talking 'bout, *I made fifteen hundud dollas las night.* I told her good, now you can buy some cream for dat so ass of yawn. Uh-hmm, I show did," Mrs. Matty said, adding a new dip to her lip. "Tell me she makin' friends wit dem lil flippin' fellas they be showin' on television from time to time. Dey got a place where dey put on shows. Den, she go to poddys wit dem transexes and thangs", she added.

The months passed quickly. Glammer and Jontavious were spending more and more time with Enrique at his apartment in Trenton Hills. Enrique had bought Jontavious a race car shaped bed. The sheets and comforter all had race cars and car numbers all over it. He'd decorated the walls with super hero decals and told Jontavious that it was his room whenever they were there. Enrique even paid for the child to attend the expensive on-site child care facility in the apartment community when they lived.

On Saturdays, the three of them would join the busy shopping mob at the local mall, only stopping to have lunch at a sit-down restaurant. Glammer was not used to that at all. He hardly ever took them to any of those cheesy fast food places with the supposedly tasty burgers.

To complicate her life even more, Jontavious was learning to talk and he had started calling Enrique daddy. Although Enrique seemed to enjoy his new nickname, Glammer was a little uncomfortable. *What if Johnny showed up and taye-taye is calling someone else daddy? What will happen if Enrique and Johnny end up fighting over taye-taye's paternity. It doesn't matter, she thought, Enrique was doing more for the both of them than Johnny ever had. Then again, Johnny was younger and he left us. He just went away. He skipped town before he was to appear in court, after I spent all of my everything to get him out of jail.* She fought back and forth with her feelings, but was soon able to put everything to rest following a trip to the emergency room doing the night. Glammer called Anna Rosa from the emergency room and told her that she was pregnant that she'd be an hour late for work.

Two days later, Enrique and Glammer took Jontavious to daycare. Everything was going well, Enrique dropped Glammer off at The Nitecap motel and went on to start his vending deliveries. When Glammer told Enrique that she was pregnant, he insisted that she and Jontavious move in with him permanently. Glammer wasn't sure what to do or even if she should. She wasn't sure that she was ready to move. Anna Rosa was such a good friend. She hadn't even mentioned the fact that everyone was talking about the slight weight gain that was first noticed by Spicey, just before Mrs. Matty picked up on it. The way Anna Rosa figured it, whether Glammmer was pregnant or just gaining weight, it was Glammer's business. Darvell and her four sons were Anna Rosa's business. Glammer, on the other hand was her friend and she'd always seen potential in her, and if Glammer needed her help, she'd be there.

Anna Rosa was a firm believer in the fact that sometimes you've gotta give a little push, then stand back and see what happens. She'd given Glammer that push when she got her hired at the motel. Everything else was up to Glammer. She had faith in her friend from the moment she showed up at Rosita's party. Glammer wanted a better life and Anna Rosa knew that somehow, she would achieve her dream. It was lunchtime at the motel. All the housekeepers were standing around the table about to engage in a pot luck as they waited for Glammer to bring in the apple pie.

Sticking her head out the door, Spicey yelled in Glammer's direction, "Comon 'lil girl, aint nobody got all day!"

When Anna Rosa saw Glammer walking in, she immediately ran over to greet her, "Hey girlfriend, what's been happen with you these day?", she asked.

"Dig in honey', Mrs. Matty told her,' I got a pot of turkey necks, potatos and green beans fresh off the stove. Good ole fashioned hot water cornbread right here."

" Yeah, cause I thank we ALL can see what's been happ'n with you these days", Spicey said, nodding her head towards Glammer's slightly showing tummy.

Anna Rosa gave Spicey a quick threatening look, "try the turkey necks Spicey', lowering her voice she added, 'maybe it'll shut you up a while."

Spicey put the meat in her mouth, being careful not to smudge her lipstick while glearing her eyes towards Anna Rosa and, wriggling her neck as if she was charming a snake. It was obvious that she thought she was so much better than everyone else because she always had a pocketful of money and the latest designer jeans that she managed to paint on everyday with the skimpiest blouses. Her wigs along must have cost at least three hundred dollars a piece. The diamond rings were suppose to have been gifts from satisfied customers. The pungent colognes and pefumes supposedly cost over seventy-five dollars and ounce, but they smelled more like they cost about three dollars a bottle.

"I'm moving to Trenton Hills!" Glammer told Anna Rosa.

"Don't worry though, I'm still keeping my job here for awhile, 'cause I have to pay for my classes at Trenton Hills Tech". She told Anna Rosa excitedly.

"OOOh girl!', Anna Rosa said yelled, 'you gotta tell me all about it. You comin' home to pack tonight?", she asked.

Not hearing anything other than the fact that Glammer was moving to Trenton Hills, Spicey, yanked her head back in surprise and stood up for clarification. Tapping Glammer on the shoulder she asked, "Lil girl, I know I didn't hear you right. Did you just say you movin' to Trenton Hills?"

"Yeah, this weekend, why", Glammer asked.

Walking over to Glammer, Spicey asked, "Who you thank you is, Patty Whitegirl?" She looked at Glammer from head to toe, "We caint afford to live out there 'round all dem white folks, and I got news for ya sista girl,' Uncle Sam aint footin' the rent for ya to live there!"

"If you brang yo head up every now and then, you'da know her mane live out there", Mrs. Matty told her.

"I had about enough of you, heffer', Spicey told Mrs. Matty,' I'd hate to have to kick an old lady's ass.(she paused) You know what I mean bitch?"

Feeling a bit threatened, Mrs. Matty started rocking back and forth, and biting on her bottom lip as if she had her dip in. She reached in her bag and pulled out a seven inch barber's razor. Slinging it open she told Spicey, "I CUT yo' ass!"

"Yo old ass all up in my mix, have you told on Dawvell yet?" she asked, bobbing her head side to side. "Yeah', she added, 'tell that!"

She walked over by Anna Rosa who was standing by the doorway. Making eye to eye contact with her, she turned and looked at Mrs. Mattie. "Gone, Mrs. Clara Matty', gone and tell how you sees Dawvell coming in here every other day to fuck that white girl that used to work her."

Turning back to look at Anna Rosa, with a smirk on her face, she said, "Tells me he rents the honeymoon suite and buy rose petals and shit for her."

She turned back to smiled at Mrs. Matty, "Ain't that right Clara Matty?", she asked.

"When you move to Trenton Hills, invite me over', she said to Glammer,'just make sure you're standing outside. I'll rent a helicopter and look for the lil' black speck."

She pulled a tiny bottle of perfume from her cleavage and dapped some behind each ear. "Peace Out, bitches!", she said as she walked out the door.

Anna Rosa walked over to Mrs. Matty, who was putting her blade back in her bag. "We cool Mrs. Matty, 'she told her as she leaned down and planted a kiss on the old lady's cheek,' I love you, but I'm gonna kick Darvell's ass."

Mrs. Matty looked at her in confusion. "Baby, what happened to 'yo accent?"

That evening, Glammer went to Anna Rosa's house to pack her bags. Anna Rosa had just put Reko, Meko, Ja'lil and Shaquille to bed, and kissed them goodnight, when she heard pounding on the door. Looking out the window, Glammer alerted Anna Rosa that it was Darvell. He appeared to be on the phone but he was trying to hide the fact that he was talking to someone. He had no idea that Anna Rosa already knew about his relationship with Stacy.

Anna Rosa opened the door just wide enough to see what Darvell wanted.

"What you mean what I want?', he asked, as he began to push on the door,' I come to see mine. Op'n da dough woman, witcho crazy ass."

"The boys sleep Darvell', she yelled at him through the door, 'why dunchu go see Stacy, I hear she lettin' you in".

"What you mean by that!', he yelled back, 'what you mean by that!" Realizing that his little secret had been discovered, he tried to make the conversation all about the boys. He stuck his foot between the door and the frame.

"I gots rights ya'know', he said stupidly,' I gots the right to see my boys. Dat's law hure in Amurrica. A mane can see his kids!" Suddenly, as if a shreak of terror flashed through his body, he started banging even harder on the door and trying to force his way inside.

"You bannot have no uttha mane in there, I know dat!", he warned. Anna Rosa opened the door slightly wider, giving him hope, then she slammed it back in place so hard that it nearly broke his foot as he yanked it out screaming. "Oh, oh, so now you try'n to lame me, huh?', he cried out in pain,' now you try'n to lame me!"

His phone started ringing. It was Stacy so he backed away from the door so that he could answer in private. He was unaware that Anna Rosa could still hear his side of the conversation.

"Na'll baby. I just wanted to see my boys ba'fo dey went to bed. I know it's after ten baby. Na'll, now see, it ain't even like dat. I told you shone mean nothing' to me. Na'll , now look, now, she just my babies momma. Look, I be over in a frew minutes. Aw'ight."

Angrily, Anna Rosa opened the door to confront Darvell. "That was Stacy, wasn't it?,' she asked him, 'well, she can have you. Don't come over her no more Darvell."

"Don't be ackin' me who was on my phone' ,he told her,' dis my phone. You aint got no bitness disrespectin' me like that! Now open this damn dough!"

Darvell busted through the door, knocking Anna Rosa to the floor.

"Oma 'bouta teach yo' ass some respect. Oma mane, you s'pose da treat me like a mudda fuckin' kane, ho!', he yelled, as he immediately jumped on top of her and started slapping her so hard that he left full hand prints across her face.

Glammer had called the police when she heard the door crash open.

In the back room, she waited for help to arrive while trying to hold back four little boys who were worried about their mother. While trying to keep Meko and Reko in bed, Ja'lil and Shaquille managed to escape her grasp and went running in the living room, throwing toys and swinging jumbo baseball bats at Darvell. Between kicking and scratching and trying to get away from him, Anna Rosa called out to the boys In Spanish telling them to go back to their bedrooms and stay with their brothers.

Doing as she asked, the boys ran back to the bedroom screaming and crying.

Hearing her tell them something in a language he couldn't understand angered Darvell even more. "What the hell you tell them?", he asked her. He grabbed her by the throat with one hand and punched her in the face with his fist. "Don't be teachin' my boys dat shit', he screamed at her, splattering saliva all over her face, 'dey Amurrcan. Dey gon speak Amurrcan!"

All the domestic violence came to an end, in a split second, as six police cars swirled into the driveway. "Hole up!, hole up!, hole up mane!" Darvell yelled, as two police officers were beating him over the head and back with nightsticks.

"I just wonna see my boys.", he told them.

"They can visit you in jail.", one of the officers told him

"Aw'ight, mane, Aw'ight, Awight, Aw'ight, damn!', can I at least pull my damn pansis back up. Y'all got my ass hanging all out and shit." One of the officers yanked the back of his belt in an attempt to help him pull up his sagging jeans.

Darvell was thrown in the backseat of one of the squad cars, where he sat, while Anna Rosa filed charges against him. The next day she went to the police station to file a restraining order. Soon after, Darvell became a faded memory.

CHAPTER THREE

Stank Stanks Back in Town

"*Say what? Stank Stank in town! Lilly, ain seen dat boy in so long. Now he right smart olda than Spicey, ain't he? (pausing) Only two years? Uh-hmm, now him and Spicey ain't gat da same daddy 'cause Julldeen was married at one point. I b'leeve she was married to Stank Stank daddy. Uh-hmm, I knowed she run him off. She run crazy fooling ran with Spicey daddy. Stank Stank claim any dem kids he got? Fo aw five of dem lil big head boys look just like him. Spitting image. Heh, heh, heh! Tell me he leave a trail of babies everywhere he go.*

Look here Lilly. Stank Stank know he use da tickle me! School would be letting out for the summa time, and all the neighborhood boys be talking about gett'n dem a summa job, so dey can make dem some money. I be see-ing Stank Stank walk'n home on the last day of school, I holla out tu'em, Hey Stank Stank, boy you gonna get you a job dis summa, help yo momma out some? Stank Stank used to look up at me and say," No ma'am, Mrs. Matty. My mama all right. Daddy still come 'round.

He was so carefree and mamble, couldn't help but to like him. Den he took at hanging out with Judo. You 'memba him? (pause) You memba Judo, he moved in my yeer the end of Summa wit his momma from Chicauggo or somewhere.

Started telling Stank Stank he needed a real girlfriend. You know it's Judo fault that fast tail girl he use ta hang 'round got pregnutt. Judo gave him the runcout,

and ain't told him nothing'. The girl mama went to court and had 'em all tested for paternity and when it came back Stank Stank baby, I asked him, Stank Stank how many mo babies you havin'?, he said, "Mrs. Matty, Ain havin' no mo'. Dat's

it! I gotta give up my Summa and get a job so that girl's baby can get some diapers." Lilly, what was Stank Stank real name? I know dey name da baby after him. (she paused) Dats right, Mawcell. Mawcell Robinson. (she paused)

Spicey?, child Spicey doin' the same ole thang. Talking 'bout she gonna expand her bitness to west side of Chinatown where all dem rich china men live. You know da ones dat run dem stowes and thangs. (she paused)

Lilly, Child that lil girl there, dat Glammer, I almost forgot about her since she ain't work'n at the motel no mo. Well, you know I told you she got that mixed mane, baby now. She done moved in wit 'em, out there in Trenton Hills, and they got a lil girl together. Name her ah, ah, Altina. Altina Marie Tekzonni. Tell me dey named da baby after the mane's favorite uncle Albert. Dey call him big Al. Dat baby 'bout fo months now. Oh yeah, Um-humm, Glammer and Anna Rose still friends. Sometime Anna Rosa keep dat baby while Glammer go to school. Yeah child, she takin' some kinda class over at that fancy Trenton Hill College. Alright, well, ain gonna hold ya. (she paused) Okie Dokie. Bye bye."

Anna Rosa unwrapped the plastic twist tie and slapped six beef patties on the grill. She checked the charcoal and added hickory chips that eventually masked the neighborhood's original unrecognizable evening aroma. The cookout was underway. Babies and toddlers ran around giggly and cheerful as they played with various lawn toys and ate melting ice cream while trying to savage several drips streaming down their sticky little arms. Rosita, Anna Rosa's cousin, pranced around eating unusual food combinations while proudly displaying her five month pregnancy under a paisley halter top that matched her flip flops and sun visor.

Mrs. Matty was lounging on the plastic recliner near the CD player that was blasting a variety of Latin party songs through powerful mini speakers.

"Anna Rose', Mrs. Matty called out,' aint Glammer comin' to yo poddy?" She sipped the sparkling wine cooler and burped long and loudly. "Oooh Child, 'cuze me! I thank dez little dranks gettin' to me. Um-hmm, dey show tasty though."

Laughing at the sight of the relaxing old lady, Anna Rosa responded, "She should be here any minute Mrs. Matty. She had to drive Enrique to the airport."

"Dipping a potato chip in bean dip, Mrs. Matty asked, "Why she takin' him to the airport, he got some people comin' to town?"

"No', Anna Rosa answered as she flipped the burgers,' Enrique is going out of town for a vending conference."

"I guess she be here directly than.", Mrs. Mattie mummured as she took another swig from the wine cooler bottle. Her attention quickly changed to the small sparkly dark blue car with gold spinners that swooped up to Anna Rosa's house blocking the driveway. *Dat fool there don't know how to drive,* she thought as she starred at the vehicle in an attempt to see who was hiding behind the driver's dark tinted window.

"You babies come back up dis way!", she yelled out, making sure the children were a safe distance from the strange vehicle.

A few seconds later, the front passenger door opened and Spicey got out wearing her lastest wig. It was shoulder length, curly and blond. She'd sprayed nealy a half can of hair spray on it, trying to make the cheap synthetic hair appear real. Mrs. Matty shook her head negatively, "Dat child know black folk ain't got no blond hair", she said quietly. "Clara Matty!,' Spicey called out, 'Dis Stank Stank. My brother". Just then the driver side window came down to reveal a neat bearded young man, wearing a dressy designer leather hat and sunglasses. He waved at her.

"Lawdy Mercy!', she shouted, 'Stank Stank! Dat's lil Stank Stank?" She walked over closer to the car for a closer look.

"Boy get out dat ca'n give Mrs. Matty a hug!", she commanded. Stank Stank got out of the car and stood next to Mrs. Matty, as she gave him a once over.

"Look at you', she said,' got yoself a lil ole beard, lookin' all fine and thangs!"

"How you doin' Mrs. Matty?", he finally asked while leaning over to give the old woman a kiss on the cheek. Still hugging him around the waist, she looked up and attempted a whistle, "Fine young mane you turned out to be!"

"Thank you, Mrs. Matty", Stank Stank said as he smiled widely displaying gold teeth all across the front of his mouth. Not approving of his alteration, Mrs. Matty starred suspiciously, "Boy, what da hell you done done to yo' malf?, she asked, 'lookin' like a damn fool."

"I'm stylin' and profilin' Mrs. Matty", he told her respectfully. Stank Stank always tried to be a nice decent individual around Mrs. Matty because it had been said that she used to baby sit him when he was just a newborn. Then as he grew older, he could always stop by Mrs. Matty's house for a peanut butter and Jelly sandwich and a glass of

milk. He also was friends with her son, June bug, who was now working in landscaping with Judo.

Pulling him by the hand, she asked, "You stayin' for da potty? We
got hamburgers and fried pickles, good tastin' lil dranks and ish
cream." Slowly pulling away from her and making his way toward the
idling car, he said, "No maam, I just dropped Spicey off. I gotta roll
Mrs. Matty, I might come by a little later."

She winked and nodded at him as he drove alway. *Now, why caint
Spicey be mo' like her brother,* she thought. Spicey had just changed the
music from Latin to rhythm and blues when Glammer drove into the
driveway. They could see the top of Jontavious's head as he strained to
see outside the car, while his baby sister Altina sucked contently on a
pacifier. Mrs. Matty had fallen asleep, but was soon awakened by the
slamming of car doors and shouting of excitement, from the twins, as
they ran to the car and welcomed Jontavious. They were excited to
show him all the lawn toys they had just waiting to be played with.
Jontavious, having skipped lunch due to the trip to the airport, got
away from the boys as soon as he could and ran over to Anna Rosa
who happily gave him a hug and a kid- sized cheeseburger. She then
put a few hot dogs on the grill and was about to walk over to Glammer; who still hadn't left the car with the baby. In the distance she
could see Spicey leaning on the hood of the car with her butt stuck up
in the air. She was slinging her ugly, fake blond hair around and smiling like she do when she's about to make some special money. It almost
looked like Spicey was trying to be friends with Glammer. Suspiciously, Anna Rosa picked up three coolers and headed towards the car.
"What up, my sistas", she said while handing each girl a wine cooler.

"Hey Anna Rosa". Spicey snapped off. She took the cooler and
quickly turned her attention back towards Glammer. Feeling uneasy
about Spicey hanging around Glammer, Anna Rosa decided to stay

awhile. "You ain't married to dat boy yet, and Stank Stank just need somebody to go to da potty with him. Since all dem singers and rappers gonna be there, everybody gotta be in pairs", Spicey told Glammer.

Trying to get out of the talk with Spicey, Glammer asked, " Why would I want to go ANYWHERE with someone named Stank Stank?" Spicey gave her a dumb founded look, "Stank Stank a nick name lil girl, his name Mawcell", she said while sighing. Anna Rosa bumped Glammer on the arm, "What up, 'she inquired,' you look confused." Spicey gave a mind your own business look that Anna Rosa totally ignored. Rosita turned up the radio and called Anna Rosa and Glammer over for a quick dance routine. Much to Spicey's dismay, Glammer told her she'd think about it. The girls joined Rosita and Mrs. Matty who was busy doing the bump, then the motorcycle.

"Mrs. Matty still got it, ain't she, uh-hmm, hid is", she said, while sticking out her bottom and pretending to turn handles on a motorcycle as she jerked her shoulders in beat with the music. Meanwhile Spicey was busy creating her own lap dance for a group of guys, who just happened to walk pass Anna Rosa's house. Since Spicey was distracted from Glammer for a while, Anna Rosa

Pulled her aside.

"What up with you girlfriend?', she asked, 'you buddy buddy with Spicey all of a sudden."

"No!', Glammer said in protest, 'she want me to go with her brother to a party for her. She was going to go with him, but she's got a chance to get hooked up making money over in Chinatown".

"What she thinking', Anna Rosa asked, 'she know you got babies". Anna Rosa noticed a hint of curiosity about Glammer.

"You want to go to this party?", she asked.

"She said it's a backstage kind of thing, but you can't go unless you're with someone', Glammer explained,' I've never been to a real party before and Enrique is out of town for a couple days. It might be fun. If you can't watch Taye Taye and Tina, I guess I can ask Mrs. Matty".

"Good enough girl! Just keep an eye on that Stank Stank, he came by here earlier and if it wasn't for the gold grille and his height, he might be an attractive guy!', she said,' but still be on your guard, he is Spicey's brother. Oh, and about a baby sitter, you don't need Mrs. Matty, I am Auntie Anna."

The Nitecap motel was considered neutral territory. Anytime the employees wanted to meet up with someone they didn't know, they'd arrange a meeting in the lobby or somewhere in the parking lot. Glammer didn't know Stank Stank. She didn't know that while she was working at the motel, that Stank Stank knew Mrs. Matty, or that he and Spicey grew up in the same neighborhood as did Johnny and Judo. She didn't even know, at that time, that Spicey even had siblings! It was like Glammer's mom rented that house after all ties were broken. Maybe that's why the only person she really trusted was Anna Rosa.

Glammer sat in the car waiting for Spicey to show up with her brother Stank Stank. Instead she saw Spicey get into the front seat of an expensive vehicle across the street and literally disappear. Feeling somewhat disappointed, she got out of the car to meet up with Anna Rosa who should've been just about to have lunch. In route to the lobby, she heard someone running behind her. She turned suddenly to see what it was all about. Walking up behind her, seemingly at a mile a second, was a short, stocky, man smelling of dirt and cheap stale cologne. He was wearing clothing that appeared three times his regular size and had a gold looking chain around his neck that held a huge dollar sign. His beard was neatly trimmed and his mouth looked as though he had just rubbed moisturizer on his lips. Glammer decided to pause at the newpaper machine in an attempt to get out of this his way. Unfortunately, while she was putting coins in the machine, she saw a large black patent imitation leather shoe appear right beside her. She tried to hurry so that she could go inside the motel to safety. The character standing next to her didn't say anything, but what she didn't realize was, he was silently sizing her up. After she bend down and got the newspaper, she heard a deep dragging voice.

"Hey baby', it said,' What yo' name is?" Not getting an answer right away, he threw in, "Look at ya. Pruddy lil thang, I bet you wait'n here for me aint ya?"

"I don't think so!", Glammer said sarcastically.

" Ah, don't be like dat girl', he said, 'I heard you was nice."

Silently feeling like she wanted to turn and expectorate her breakfast, Glammer tried to speak, "Youre not. Oh please tell me your'e not him."

Smiling, as if he 'd just won a major prize in a contest, he answered.

"Fo Sho!" He moved closer and brushed his shoulder against hers.

"Om Mawcell . My sister Spicey said om takin' you to a porty baby", he told her.

Looking like she wanted to faint, she asked suddenly, "You're not wearing that are you?"

"Girl, you funny', he said, smacking his lips like he was tasting something deliciously sweet for the first time, 'but it ain't no thang', he scanned her from head to toe, while squinting his mascara lined eyes,' I can deal." He started nodding approvingly. About that time Spicey came running across the street, stuffing something into her bra and holding onto her wig.

"Stank Stank you ready to go to lunch?", Spicey asked, as she got closer.

"Mawcell. Spicey damn!', he told her,' Om tryin' da lay my mack on and you gonna call me some Stank Stank; Sistagirl dat's like me comin' over knockin' on dat ca winda when you was takin' care yo bitness.", he told her.

"Aint nobody but her!', Spicey said pointing her head toward Glammer', 'shaint nobody!"

"Yown know dat dough, he said,' trying to eye Glammer seductively, 'dis sweet lil thang might be yo sista law."

Leaving the newspaper on top of the newstand, Glammer held up both hands. "I've gotta go.", she said making a mad dash for her car.

Stank Stank turned and followed Glammer half way to her car.

"Tomorrow night baby, okay, right hure. You and me 'bout eight. Okay baby. I holla!", he yelled to her as she drove away.

Glammer went home and reluctantly started making plans to attend the party with Marcell. *Spicey's gonna owe me big for this one,* she thought. She washed, dried and curled her hair then experimented with several make up colors. She thought about going hoochie style to compliment Marcell, but soon realized that the shortest dress she owned wasn't short enough. She tried to do the painted on jeans look, but soon realized that it wasn't her. Besides, she wasn't dating Marcell so why should she care if he approved of what she looked like. He liked her earlier and she'd done nothing special, and it was going to stay that way. She decided to go dressy casual.

Finally, she layed out a pair of diamond and onyx stud earrings that Enrique had given her after Altina was born. She walked into the nursery and checked on the sleeping baby. Trying not to awaken her, she opened the closet and got the large diaper bag. It already had various baby toys inside and coloring books and crayons for Jontavious. All she had to do was stock a good supply of diapers and clothes.

When Glammer and Marcell arrived at the party, it seemed like everyone there was some kind of singer or rapper. All the rappers were wearing the latest in saggy ghetto fashion and all the singers, male and female, were dressed in expensive looking suites and dresses. Not a single person was seen flaunting anything less than diamonds and twenty-four caret gold jewelry. The music was loud and the bass was almost unbearable, but still it was somewhat entertaining. Food was layed out near every wall or partition. Glammer expected to see barbecue, fried chicken and fish. Instead she had a choice of lobster, calamari, cavier with expensive real butter crackers, or her choice of three different kinds of thick cut steak, all free for the taking. The desserts were the best. Inside a small clear refrigerator, there were slices of all kinds of liquor induced pies and cakes. There were also chunks of imported chocolates and something called herb brownies.

Marcell got lost in the crowd after being photographed with Glammer at the door, so she just wandered around looking at all the nice stuff. She enjoyed seeing the expensive artwork and statues. They were so beautiful; almost like visiting an art gallery. Every room had something. There were two billiard rooms, a poker room, a room for playing dice games and several really small rooms that looked like storage space compared to the other rooms. Glammer quickly got tired of walking around smiling and speaking to people she didn't know, so she found her way back up front to the circular couch, were several waitresses were walking around passing out drinks. She saw a mail order catalogue someone had left behind so she sat down to browse through it while sipping on some kind of mixed drink that tasted like really sweet liquid banana. It even had whip cream on top.

Appearing almost out of no where, she saw Marcell standing in front of her smiling and looking glassy eyed. He politely asked her to dance. Glammer finally was starting to enjoy the party. The more she danced with Marcell, the more guys asked her to dance with them. It was getting late and Glammer was tiring. Marcell

Cut in and took her down the hall to a smaller room with a movie screen and went back for drinks. She was curious as to what movie they were going to see. When he came back, they talked while sipping Champaign. He was being such a gentleman that Glammer totally forgot that he was Spicey's brother.

They talked about current movies and news, and her likes and dislikes. They talked about her children and his children. They even talked about their families. It was then that Glammer realized that he knew Johnny and his brother Judo. Marcell had no idea that Johnny had fathered her son Jontavious. He told her that after his son was born, he left town to get a better job so that he could send money home and lost track of everybody except for Spicey and his mom. He even told her about how Mrs. Matty baby-sat him and gave him lunch when he was a little boy. Glammer thought that if nothing else, they would become good friends.

It appeared that underneath his ignorant, good for nothing ways, he was actually a nice guy. Since the room they were in was sound proof, instead of watching a movie, he put in a CD full of old original music from the 80's and they danced and talked nearly all night, only stopping to allow him enough time to refill their glass and grab a tray of food. Right then, at that party, in that room, it was like she'd found the brother she'd never had. Then they started to play cards, first spades, then gin and then something went terribly wrong.

Glammer woke up the next morning laying on the sofa with a blanket over her. In shock she jumped up only to find Marcell standing over by the door, wearing nothing but a towel around his waist, and talking on his cell phone. She quickly searched the room for her clothes and got dressed as Marcell hung up the phone.

"Hole up baby girl' ,he said, 'why you runnin'?"

Glammer was extremely dizzy and wasn't standing very steadily. She started to fall backwards and Marcell rushed over and caught her just as she was about to bang her head.

"You really need to sit down a while. Let me go get us some pancakes, eggs and bacon and shit.", he told her

He grabbed the keys to the SUV, and was going towards the door when she realized that he'd gotten her keys off the table and they'd supposed to have been in her purse. Feeling extremely embarrassed she asked, "What happened, what did you do to me?"

"Ain did nothin' you ain't want me to do baby", he lied.

"Give me my keys!", Glammer shouted.

"Ah, it's like dat now, huh?', he said,' you get yo lil fix to remind you what it's like bein' wit a real brotha, then you gone."

Glammer didn't answer him. She grabbed her purse and rushed out the door. Nearly everyone had left except the waitresses and the clean up crew. Marcell followed her shouting.

"Gone din bitch!', he yelled at her,' I shoulda put yo ass out last night and got wit a real woman and not somebaddy who want a caramel dipped white boy!"

Glammer drove straight to Anna Rosa's house to pick up her children and try to explain why she hadn't picked them up last night after the party. Wiping tears away and cleaning her nose at every stop light along the way, she thought about Enrique and how he had asked her to marry him when she dropped him off at the airport. He was due back soon. Glammer knew she should be happy about it but instead she felt guilty, sad , dirty and sore. She needed someone to talk to, someone who could help her decide what to do.

When she arrived at Anna Rosa's, the house looked completely still, like no one was home. Perhaps they were still asleep. She unlocked the door, walked inside and sat on the sofa putting her head in her hands trying to relieve her pounding headache. Glammer had nearly dozed off when Mrs. Matty emerged from a back bedroom.

"Lawdy Mercy!", she screamed, not expecting to see anyone sitting on the sofa. "Child, I thought you was a haint!," she said fanning her face. Mrs. Matty clenched her chest and started rubbing. Now able to smile, Mrs. Matty said, "Om sho dat my'neer gave old Mrs. Matty a heart attack fo sho."

Glammer leaped to her feet, staggering, to make sure Mrs. Matty was okay. After their breathing returned to normal, Mrs. Matty took a good long look at Glammer, noticing the worn, wrinkled and stained dress, her muzzled hair and day old make-up. Glammer quietly returned to the sofa. Mrs. Matty got a pot of coffee started, while still keeping an eye on Glammer who looked like she'd been drug in by the cat. She rinsed out two mugs, keeping them separate. In the mug intended for Glammer, she added a little cream and sugar.

Making sure she was out of sight, she pulled a small bottle of vodka from her robe pocket and poured a few ounces in her mug to add with her coffee. She returned with the coffee and handed the virgin cup to Glammer. Trying to pretend that her blood-shot eyes were from lack of sleep, Glammer faked a good, long yawn. Not being fooled by her actions, Mrs. Matty said," Um-hmm. Drank yo coffee baby." Glammer drank the warm refreshing liquid, eventually quenching her dessert dry throat.

"Good, ain't it?', Mrs. Matty asked,' I likes it strong myself."

Feeling somewhat better, Glammer started to talk.

"Where's Anna Rosa?', she asked. Mrs. Matty pulled some tobacco from her robe pocket, broke off a hunk, put it in her mouth and positioned it properly in her lip. She took a deep breath.

"Anna Rose gone to the hospital with Rosita 'bout nine last night.' Moving the tobacco chunk around to gain moisture she continued, 'she called me over to keep a eye on dem babies." Finding her stuffed foam cup on the side of the sofa, Mrs. Matty picked it up and added some more tissue to the bottom.

"You got sumptn' you want to talk about sugga?", Mrs. Matty asked.

Glammer tried to get up and go check on the boys, but Mrs. Matty pulled her back.

"Mrs. Matty, I don't want to get into this right now, okay?", Glammer told her.

Mrs. Matty cleared the brown liquid from her mouth and took a sip of her coffee. "You don't get into it now, baby, it still gon be there later." she said.

Glammer couldn't think straight, it hurt too much, but she did manage to realize that she couldn't afford to wait for Anna Rosa. She had a lot to get accomplished before Enrique returned, especially now. The fear and worry was showing on her face.

"Glammer listen here a minute", Mrs. Matty told her. Glammer took one look at the sincere old lady and busted into tears.

"You gonna tell Mrs. Matty what happened at dat potty last night and we gon keep it between us. You hear me child?", Mrs. Matty commanded.

"I can't Mrs. Matty', Glammer hesitated,' it involves someone you know and I don't want you to have to pick sides."

Mrs. Matty sipped her vodka induced coffee accidentally mixing it with tobacco juice already brewing in her mouth. She frowned, grabbed her foam cup and got rid of all the juices. Then she sipped her coffee again.

"Let Mrs. Matty tell you what she know.", she told Glammer

"I know you went to dat potty with Stank Stank. I know he Spicey's brotha. I can go on and on. You see, there aint too much Mrs. Matty don't know. Now seems to me, you got yo'self a real live problem. Anna Rosa aint here. By the time she get here, it may be too late. Right now Sugga, Mrs. Matty all you got, "she explained.

Taking a deep breath and trying to fight back tears, Glammer explained what happened at the party. She explained how glassy Marcell's eyes looked and how nice and polite he was. She explained how she must have blacked out because she couldn't remember anything more except waking up with the blanket.

"I don't want you to have to take sides', Glammer said again,' see why I need Anna Rosa.?" Mrs. Matty leaned back, "Baby you need Anna Rose, cause you wont Anna Rose. Wontin' ain't needing. Wont'n Wont'n.", you understand what om sayin'?" Mrs. Matty added to the foam cup again, then sipped her coffee.

"You right. I been knowing Stank Stank since he was born. I know he got babies spread out 'bout fo diff'rent states. How he got 'em, I caint rightly say, but if he got'em the way you say thangs happened with you, we need to call the po'east. Mrs. Matty know Stank Stank. He dat hot, stankin' fast Spicey's brotha. Mrs. Matty know Glammer too. She good people. Now you dry dem tills", Mrs. Matty lectured. Just before Anna Rosa returned home, the police arrived at her house to take a statement from Glammer. She was then transported to the hospital where they found traces of a drug in her blood. Later that day as Glammer slept and Anna Rosa watched the boys, Spicey's brother Stank Stank was being arrested.

"You need to talk to Glammer when she wake up, Anna Rose", Mrs. Matty said.

Paying no attention to the old lady, Anna Rosa said," OOh wait a minute Mrs. Matty, look at the news brief. Spicey's brother Stank Stank in jail!". She said.

I wonder what he did, she thought.

CHAPTER FOUR

Where is Spicey?

Mrs. Matty took a small, brand new cellular phone out of her pocket and called her best friend Lilly.

"Hey Lilly, what you know?", Mrs. Matty asked.

"I know you figured out how to use dat cauless phone Matty", Lilly replied.

"See, dis ain't no coddless phone', Mrs. Matty said,' dey call it wy-less.

"I hear ya Matty, try'n to keep up with young folk . Spicey been looking for you", she told her.

"What she wont wit me?', Mrs. Matty said, ' ain got no bitness wit her".

"I thank she wonna take you over and let you see that 'poddment she got in the valley near Chinatown.", Lilly responded.

" 'Poddment, huh?', Mrs. Matty listened.

"Yeah, she took me by there this mornin', it's a nice area. She got a good view of the Chinatown Shopping Mall.' ,Lilly explained, 'the poddment easy to fine. It's a small complex called Oak Square. She said now she can hand wash her 'spensive draws and thangs and hang 'em ova da balcony to air dry. So when you go, just look for dem lil red ho draws on the balcony." Lilly laughed.

"Uh!', Mrs. Matty commented,' aint even moved in good yet, and already makin' it ugly, hanging her little nasty draws all out over the balcony where folks can see 'em."

"That girl got a phone call and got me home in five minutes. she was drivin' so fast, said her brother Stank Stank was in jail for sumpt'n call date rape. She had to come up 'bout fitteen hundud to bail him out.", Lilly reported.

"Sho nuff?", Mrs. Matty asked.

"Yeah, but she say shaint worried cause she got a poddy in China-town dis weekend, say she getting' paid five thousand dollars!", Lilly told Matty.

"Uh-hmm', some 'ho poddy", Mrs. Matty said.

"I assa how she gone make dat kind of money in just one day?', Lilly said,' and she told me it was a two night group poddy. Next thang I knowed, she was drivin' down da street. Justa speed'n."

"Uh-hmm, yeah.', Mrs. Matty said,' I gotta go now Lilly. Cook'n me some beans and turkey nakes, don't wonna messit up. Okie Doke! Bye-bye." forty eight hours passed quickly. Glammer and the children had spent the entire weekend with Anna Rosa. After Glammer filled her in on what happened at the party with Marcell, Anna Rosa became tremendously upset.

"We should go kick both their asses, right now!", she screamed.

Then she grabbed her car keys and spent nearly five minutes rambling something in Spanish. Calming down, she switched back to English.

"Watch the children,' she said, 'I've gotta get out of here before I frighten them."

Chasing her out of the house, Glammer asked," Where are you going?"

Did she really need to ask that question? Glammer though.

Anna Rosa stopped for a split second and turned around. You could see the blood boiling in her face.

"Girlfriend', she replied, taking took a deep breath, 'I don't know."

Anna Rosa picked up an iron baseball bat from the side of the house, got in her car and drove away, blasting the radio.

Glammer was changing Altina when the cell phone rang. It was Enrique. He was due back at the airport in thirty-five minutes and she had to get six kids into shoes and socks, making sure five of them used the bathroom before being put in the car and strapped down. It was a difficult task, but she managed. The trip to the airport was even worse. Wearing some jeans, he had on two days before, Jalil found a stale burrito and started munching on it. When Meko saw him eating the stale burito, he tried to take it away and discard of it.

Ja'lil, not wanting to give up his snack, forced half the burrito into his mouth. Unfortunately, the remaining half ended up on the floor of the SUV. Approaching a red light, Altina dropped her pacifier, Shaquille unbuckled his seatbelt to pick it up. Meko unbuckled his seatbelt to help and Altina got impatient and started crying. Jontavious, wanting to make sure Glammer knew that he was watching his baby sister, yelled, "Mama, Tina crying!"

Getting frustrated, she said, " Thank you Taye Taye, I hear her."

By the time she made it to the airport, Enrique had just walked out and was looking for her.

"There's daddy!', Jontavious shouted, unbuckling his seat belt and bouncing on the seat. "Daddy, daddy, daddy", he said over and over again.

"Taye-Taye. Quiet! Stop that bouncing and get back in your seat belt." Glammer commanded. Enrique got in the truck and everything seemed to settle down a bit, but not for long. The stale burrito had given Ja'lil gas. The boys started laughing and pushing all the buttons trying to get the windows down. Enrique smirked at the brief thought of them as teenagers and assisted in getting the window down.

Meko, the older twin had stopped laughing and started twanting his brother.

"Ja'lil, your pig! Pig, pig, pig, pig, dirty farting pig", he yelled. Ja'lil being of the younger set of twins didn't like being called a pig and started crying as the twanting continued.

With all the chatter and commotion in the back seats getting to her, Glammer pulled over to the side of the road. "Meko', 'she tried to say calmly,'please stop calling your brother a pig."

Enrique unbuckled his seat belt. "Let me drive okay", he asked. Just then, Meko started started calling his brother a pig again, but this time, he done so in Spanish expecting to get away with it. To his surprise, Enrique got back out of the car and opened the door to the SUV. He looked straight at Meko.

"Call him a pig one more time', he said sternly,' and youre going to be in big trouble young man." The remaining ride home was so quiet that Glammer and Enrique had no trouble listening to the radio at a low peaceful level. They even heard an entire news brief that, for some reason, gave Glammer chills.

A missing persons' alert has been issued for twenty-three year old Spicey Robinson. Robinson was last seen, in China town, driving a

1987 blue compact vehicle with gold spinners. The car was found yesterday on Changway Boulevard at a gas station, and later claimed by a Marcell Robinson, owner of the vehicle and brother of Ms. Robinson. Again, a missing persons' alert has been issued for twenty-three year old Spicey Robinson.

I'm Chuck Westbrier for WSDG news.

"You know, I graduate this Spring. I have an interview at Trenton Hills Memorial Hospital a week after graduation", Glammer mentioned.

"Yeah!, X-ray tech', he looked over at Glammer, 'you seem a little nervous. What do you know about that news report?" He asked.

"What news report?', Glammer tried to play it off,' Oh the one about Spicey. Nothing. I didn't even know she was missing."

Enrique took the long way back to Anna Rosa's, giving the children plenty time to fall asleep. Then, he stopped by A-Tek Vending warehouse to check the morning deliveries. It was then that he asked Glammer to marry him for the second time.

"Okay I'll marry you', she answered,' but first I have to tell you something.

After checking to make sure the backseat gang was still asleep, she told Enrique all about the weekend, and Marcell and Mrs. Matty and the police. Then she mentioned the drug he'd used and her hospital experience. Through tears, she told him the whole sordid story. To her surprise, he kissed her lips and asked, "What did Anna Rosa do to Spicey?"

"I hope nothing.", she said.

"As for Marcell, I can call Big Al if he doesn't get jail time, it wont be good.", Enrique told her.

"There's no reason to get your grandfather involved", she replied.

"Grandfather? Yuck!', he stated, 'he hates to be called grandfather."

"Yeah', Glammer smiled,' I wonder why."

"No, you don't', Enrique told her, 'now, back to us, I can I adopt Jontavious".

"He calls you daddy anyway", Glammer admitted.

After dropping off Anna Rosa's boys, Glammer and Enrique headed home. They put the children to bed, and went out onto the balcony to explore the stars and planets. It was a breezy night and the sky was clear. He focused in on the Big Dipper and showed her the ring around Saturn. While looking in awe at Saturn's ring, Enrique took a tiny black leather case out of his trouser pocket and waited for Glammer's attention. When she was done exploring the night's sky, he presented her with the official symbol of their engagement. He gave her a pink sapphire ring with three rows of diamonds half way around each side of the twenty-four caret gold band. Glammer was breathless.

"If you don't breathe soon, I'm going to have to call for help", Enrique told her.

"How did you know I'd say yes", Glammer asked, still glaring at the ring that he'd placed on her finger.

"Because you didn't say no when I asked you at the airport", he told her.

Glammer couldn't take her eyes off the engagement ring. It was so beautiful and she thought it was, by far, the most expensive piece of jewelry she'd ever own.

Enrique stepped inside to check the kids and get a couple glasses of ice tea. He returned to the balcony and they sat down to enjoy the breeze on the small wicker sofa. He told her all about the convention he attented. Then he told her that his grandpa Alex was about to retire and wanted to give A-Tek vending to him as long as he didn't change the name. He explained how his grandpa started A-Tek and that it really does stand for Alex Tekzonni. He told her that when he produced a picture of Tina and the engagement ring and showed it to his grandpa, it was an instant decision. His uncle Al was originally suppose to get the company first, but he never spent time at the warehouse helping out. Enrique explained to Glammer that his grandpa believed that in order to run a successful business, you have to know what you doing and practice doing it. The night air became chilly. They went back inside just in time to see the photo of a battered face Spicey flash across the television screen, as the news anchor gave an update on her where-a-bouts.

This is an update to our story we first brought to you last night about twenty-three year old Spicey Robinson. She has been found. Repeat: The twenty-three year old female, Spicey Robinson, who was reported missing yesterday, has been found. Police was tipped off, just after midnight, to a house in the upper middle class section of Chinatown where it was said that illegal contraband was being sold. Upon raiding the property, police found a nude, battered and bruised female blindfolded, gagged and chained to what appeared to be a homemade super-sized teeter-totter. First thought to be a mail order bride, she was later identified as twenty-three year old Spicey Robinson. Ms. Robinson is recovering at a local hospital in stable condition. No one else was found on the premises. Wang Li Chu is a person of interest in this crime. For WSDG news, I'm Ginnette Cryson.

"Whoa, that's a relief.'", Glammer said, finally picking her mouth up off the floor.

"What's a relief?", Enrique asked as he returned from a quick trip to the bathroom.

Glammer looked at him inquistedly, "finding Spicey alive."

"She is a hooker trying to turn call girl', Enrique told her,'things like this happen to girls like her all the time. Fortunately, she was lucky. Most call girls without Johns to protect them aren't so lucky." He kissed her forehead.

Meanwhile, at Greenbriar Memorial, Spicey laid motionless in the hospital bed. A needle was inserted into the top of her bruised left hand. Beside the bed, hanging from a pole , was a plastic bag dripping clear liquid into a thick plastic tube. A large steel tank appeared to be pumping air into her nostrils. Something that resembled a clothes pin was clipped to her forefinger. She looked at it and sighed. Still awakening from her medicine induced nap, she moaned out in pain and glanced around the dimly lit room. The thick off-white mini blinds that covered the seemingly small window was tightly closed, preventing any sunlight from entering. In the corner set a large cozy looking recliner with a grey and red stained seat. The nearly ripped off leather, covering the arms of the chair, was now covered with blue tape that matched the shiny colored stains on the floor. It was state hospital, the rooms didn't have to be pretty, especially for the uninsured.

After being rescued from the house and taken to the ER, Spicey's appearance was anything but normal. Her once textured and moisturized weaved hair was now frezzy and dry. Pebbles of dirt from a quick washing and lice scrub still showed throughout her hairline. Her make up had been washed off and all that remained were several dark circles made by bursted pimples from years ago. An ash build up, from dry skin, covered her face and her thick bubbled lips were now flakey and peeling. The corners of her eyes were filled with dried crumbled stuff that stuck to her eyelashes and top eye lids. Feeling the crusty build up around her eyes, Spicey recalled Mrs. Matty's words from years past.

" Uh-hm, don't go 'ran lookin' like dat baby. Get dat matter out yo eyes.", she'd say. Spicey's face flashed from a look of pain to a look of annoyance at the though of the old lady. "*Helfer probably loving this.*" She remembered Mrs. Matty's thoughts about her profession. "Once a ho', always a ho'", she'd said.

" 'Ho to pro bitch", Spicey whispered to herself, 'the money's better."

Just as she began struggling to take a sip of water from the melted ice inside the luke warm pitcher beside her bed, the nurse walked in carrying a tray of medication.

"Oh now, let me help you with that', the nurse said. ' I have a fresh pitcher of ice water right here for you along with your medication." She picked up the six ounce foam cup and poured the icy water into it. Spicey nodded and whispered thank you the best she could as the nurse gently helped lean her forward, allowing her to drink from the cup.

"I have a straw some where", the nurse commented as Spicey hungrily gulped down the fluid. When She'd finished the small cup of water, the nurse reached into the pocket of her white top and pulled out three individually wrapped straws and placed it on the nightstand next to the phone.

"I have about thirty more minutes before I'm off the clock', she told Spicey,' so I suppose I can spend it in here with you tidying up a bit and trying to make the room a little more pleasant". She smiled and walked over to the small window encased in concrete and opened the blinds. The sunshine rushed into the room like a nuclear explosion. "Good Gravy!", the nurse said, while trying to adjust her eyes to the new light, 'Didn't know it was so bright out. Would you like to watch a little tv', she asked,' it's almost time for that talk show "You tha Daddy", I hear it's popular these days, she said while giving Spicey a friendly haggard smile and clicking on the television. In a news brief , the anchorman said that Wane Li Chu had been captured, but released because of a technicality.

"I'm sorry, Ms. Robinson', the nurse apologized,' I can switch channels for you." Spicey signaled no and starred bitterly at the screen.

"He'll ge-get his", she replied,' an it ain't gonna be nice." The nurse got clean bed dressings from the closet and prepared to change the bed sheets. She helped her into the patient chair and removed the two day old fitted sheet as Spicey watched the ending of the the talk show.

Across town Stank Stank had received news that he was to appear on the next taping of You tha Daddy. Even though he was to be portrayed as a dead beat dad by several of his exes, he was ecstatic because of the payment and all the freebies, not to mention the first class flight out west. Out of jail on bond, he couldn't wait to get to the hospital and brag to his sister.

Standing naked in the middle of the small dirty efficiency apartment with shower water still dripping from his body, he admired himself in the mirror. Flexing his upper body, he combed through the oddly looking patches of tightly tangled chest hair while spraying Ghetto Fabulous cologne into it, temporally streighten it out. Loud degrading rap music blarred constantly with crude language to drown out the trains that passed by his window every forty-five minutes. From time to time, other people would bang from the apartment below trying to get him to turn the music down, but he ignored them completely, only lowering the volume when he picked up his weekly, drunkened one night stand from a local sleazy bar. Stepping into and adjusting his favorite pair of once worn blue briefs, he put on a pair of nylon white track pants with a blue strip going down the side of each leg. Realizing that the blue briefs clearly showed through the white nylon track pants, he adjusted his "junk" to present the ultimate bulge. In a large cardboard box, that he used as a dresser drawer, he dug out a tight fitting blue and white ribbed tank top that showed off his rippled abdomen when tucked in. Trying to keep the waves in his hair moist, he replaced the clear shower cap on his head and covered it with a blue and white generic baseball cap. He sat on the folded down wall bed and proceeded to put on a brand new pair of Airborne Marx high top basketball shoes, that he'd bought from his friend Easy Slide. Retail value $259.00. Easy slide value, $50.00.

He grabbed a cinnamon flavored tooth pick from the coffee table that was covered with different kinds of fast food bags and old left overs, put on a pair of extra dark sunglasses, dawned his large fake gold necklace, and put a diamond earring in his ear. He gave himself a once over in a mirror that was framed in the stomach of a life sized wall hanging of an aspiring porn star.

"Murr'r, Murr'r on da wall baby', he said, moving the flavored toothpick around in the corner of his mouth, ' whose the most fly brotha of 'em all?"

He licked his dried, chapped lips and tilted down his sunglasses. Looking over the top, he winked and smiled wildly, "Tru dat! Tru dat!", he agreed.

Spicey looked at the nurse and her snug fitting white stretch pants. Her low cut blouse displayed a thin white bra which revealed her protruding nipples. Her Brunette hair was braided in a single pony tail and swirled around in a circle on top of her head. An ink pen was strategically placed diagonally through the swirled braid. Spicey thought about Stank Stank's reaction if he could see the nurse. She chuckled and turned away from the door, nodding out just as the closing theme of "You Da Daddy" played. The nurse was leaning over the bed, straightening the covers when Stank Stank approached the door. He was eating a huge double cheeseburger with lots of onions and pickles, just the way he liked it. Fully enjoying his lunch, he sported a half dry clump of mayonaise in the corner of his mouth with grease smeared across his lips. He took another bite and juices escaped the wrapping and ran down his right arm. With his mouth still full of food, he licked the juices from his arm and adjusted the paper. Partially chewing the huge bite, he packed most of it inside his left cheek, preparing to whisper out his sister's name. Instead, when he opened the door, his eyes went first to the female bent over the hospital bed, totally unaware that anyone was entering the room. Stank Stank slid in not knowing if it was Spicey's room or not, but he had to see whose rear end was sticking in the air. Not wanting to startle the woman, he stood there observing her every wiggle, twist and turn with each bite and chew, as if eating popcorn while watching a movie in a theatre. He had just finished the burger and was about to peel the wrapper off his mayo satuated hand when the nurse turned around and grabbed her chest nearing falling on top of Spicey.

"I'own mean no hum, baby', he told her smiling,' Om jest standing here watching yo' assets, and mighty fan assets dey is too." He stuck his lips out like he was whistling and wrinkled his forehead.

Still startled, the nurse was trying to conduct herself in a professional manner even though she wasn't sure who Stank Stank was. Spicey awakened, looked at the nurse and saw Stank Stank standing there.

"He my brother", she told the nurse who was in the midst of getting as far away from Stank Stank as possible.

The nurse looked at Spicey, then back at Stank Stank, trying to see the family resemblance. "I'll leave you to your visitor", she said to Spicey, while walking towards the door. Stank Stank reached out and swatted her on the rear, leaving a mustard and ketchup stain on the back of her white scrubs.

"Gotcha!", he told her, as he winked and flashed a mouthful of stained gold teeth at her. He displayed a brownish pink gum line as he made a clicking sound with his mouth, while sucking his teeth. A piece of chewed food was still plastered to his front tooth as he strolled closer to Spicey's bed.

"Whuddup 'lil sista?", he asked, helping himself to a cup of ice cold water.

Spicey looked over at Stank Stank as he picked up the cup with his still wet musturd, ketchup and mayo smeared hand.

"Have some water?",she asked sarcastically

"All girl, this ain't nuttin'. Om 'bout to blow up'. he told her,'I got it goin' on!" Spicy looked at him inquistedly.

"Ain't Miss Mattie call you yet?", he asked, forgetting the fact that Miss Mattie and Spicey aren't exactly friends. Spicey adjusted the chair to the sitting position awaiting Stank Stanks's news.

"What she gonna call me fo?", she asked, 'bitch don't like me."

Stank Stank downed the cup of water in one gulp.

"Dis some good wodda ", he told her while pouring another cup,'push dat button and tell'em you need some 'mo."

"So what you in here talking about Stank Stank?', she asked,' the only time you come talk to me all serious like is when you fixin' to do something crazy."

"Okay, gurl, check dis out', he bragged,' Om goin' to Cali. First class all da way. On one of dem big ole sev'n foddy sev'ns. Waitress lady gonna be comin' over givin' me lil bitty bottles of wine and thangs. Yo brother da shitz, Spicey', he told her, 'next thang you know, you be seein' me on "You Da Daddy".

"You Da Daddy"?, Spicey asked in amazement,' You goin' to be on You Da Daddy?"

"Damn Skippy. Deez hoes I met last Summer, when I went to out west done went and called dat show talkin' 'bout dey babies mine and shit. Anyway the mane called Mrs. Matty and told her to have me call him back. I calls him; Next thang

I know, I'm going to Callie, baby."

Spicey leaned forward with a look of concern on her face. " Stank you can't go to Callie. Hell, you cain't even leave the state! You got a court date boy!, she reminded. "Calm down gal ' ,he shushed, 'see dats the thang wit you women folk. Y'all worry too much. See, Om handling mine. I takes care of my bitness. Already talk wit Clevelle over at June's Bail Bonds and he done said dat if I leave the state, the only thang dat'll happen is dey'll try and slap me with another fine or somethin'. Da way I sees it, Om getting' two thousand dollas to appear on dat show. Dey can slap my ass via satellite. Hell Spicey, Everythang free . Hotel room at the Clearsky Suites, ya know dey got a hellified buffet. I hear dem cajun chittlins' be kickin' hawd!' ,he licked his lips and made a smacking sound.' 'Even da white folk like 'em. She-ee- it, dey throw dem austas and skrimps out da winda for some chittlins' at dis place."

"They gon be lookin' for you Stank", Spicey warned.

"Yeah, I know', he replied,' popo gon be on my ass big time, but it ain't no thang. I'll be back home befo the warrant is issued. " He leaned down and kissed her

Cheek. "Get better betsy bug", he told her as the stale smell of his lunch brushed across her face . Just hearing Stank Stank call her Betsy Bug brought back one of the few childhood memories Spicey had locked away in an old rusty footlocker. *He had just entered the third grade and was beginning to read. Spicey was barely six years old, and wanted to do everything Stank Stank done. It was Saturday morning, Stank Stank was eating a bowl of fruit crisps and reading a comic book.*

Spicey came to the table in the cutest little pink and yellow gown with matching house shoes and sleep cap.

"What you doing Stank Stank?" she asked innocently, as she climed in the chair waiting for Stank Stank to pour her a bowl of cereal. Their Grandma watched from the sink while washing dishes and humming an old negro spiritual.

"I'm reading Spicey", he told her, wishing she'd stop asking him questions.

"Can I read that paper book too", she asked him while trying to pick up the pitcher of milk.

"You too little for this book Spicey, he told her, 'you gotta read that book about that white girl and them bears like grum momma read you last night".

"Why I gotta read da baby book?,' Spicey asked,' referring to it the way Stank Stank had the day before.

Stank Stank saw Grandma glance at him over her shoulder.

"Just eat your cereal", he told her. He placed the spoon in her butterfly toddler bowl.

Late at night when everyone was in bed, Stank Stank would sneak into Spicey's bedroom and kiss her on the cheek. "Good night Betsy Bug", he'd say and run out of the room thinking no one had seen him.

"Come on', he told her,' one mo gine", he placed another peck on her cheek, leaving a splotch of saliva behind. "I holla!', he waved as he dashed towards the door trying to avoid any sentimental moments.

"Stank Stank!', Spicey yelled, stopping him at the door. ' hook me up with some 'lil bitty bottles of wine." He spun around on the the heels of his shoes, pointed two fore fingers at her and smiled wildly, crinkling his nose, "Fo Sho!"

CHAPTER FIVE
You Da Daddy

At the television studio, Stank Stank waited backstage in a room that allowed him to view the studio audience and the show's guest, at the same time, on a monitor. Instead of trying to recognize any of the women, he focused his attention on the reflection of himself in the full length mirror. He pulled at the collar of his long oversized tangerine orange pinstriped blazer, contemplating buttoning only the middle button and standing up the collar. Underneath the blazer he wore nothing but his deep dark muscular ribbed, signature chest that he had spent the last ten minutes rubbing ghetto passion man lotion all over. The oil, in the lotion, made his upper body glow with great appeal, and moistened all signs of ash, yet it produced a strong, dry woodsy smell that Stank Stank swore brought out the animal in all women in his presence.

The tangerine orange pinstripe slacks were neatly belted around his waist with a thin black belt and a large near gold flask style belt buckle that he'd already filled with gin and juice, just in case he needed a quick drink. He continued to stare in the mirror, making minor adjustments. After putting a diamond earring in his ear, and a small gold chain around his neck, he decided to leave the blazer open with a turned up collar. Finally, he stepped back to check his appearance, "Fine as wine, baby', he told himself, 'fine as wine!"

He checked his hair style and made sure his cornrows were large enough for his liking. He then put on a pair of orange and white platform shoes and dark sunglasses. Licking his front teeth for cleanliness, he sat slouched and relaxed on the leather sofa, and waited patiently for the announcement of his name.

"Ten minutes to show time, Mr. Robinson,' the stage hand warned, as he walked into the waiting room,' are we all sat?", he asked.

"Awh, yeah, mane we sat. Look hure!', Stank Stank said while standing up 'see deez', he asked, pointing to his mouth and smiling,' cleaned deez bad boys on da plain. Women folk love a mane with big pretty clean teef."

The stage hand walked farther into the room.

"What is that pungent odor?", he asked inquisively, with his nose turned in an upward wrinkle, tracing it to Stank Stank.

"Dat's Ghetto Passion Rub Me Down." Stank Stank told him proudly, as he rubbed his hands down his oiled muscular torso. Smell good don't it?". He hardened his tongue and licked it around the outside of his dry lips. 'You wonna use some?".

The stage hand moved over towards the door and got a bottle of air sanitizer out of a closet, "Oh no, no, no, no, no', he replied as he sprayed the air,' I have to be around people!" He quickly left the room holding the can tightly in his hand.

Stank Stank jumped back in shock. His face was steaming as beads of perspiration began to form on his forehead. "Oh, hell no! I know yo stank ass didn't jist call me funky!', he hollered.' You betta run yo faggot ass up outta hure, smelling like herbal funk, booty, and sugga cookies!" He walked swiftly around the room throwing punches into the air for awhile trying to calm himself down. "Ain no punk!', he screamed down the hallway while tugging at the waistline of his trousers,' I demands respect! I'll fuck you up!

Out front, he could hear the theme music playing and the audience applauding as the host took center stage surrounded by six women proudly displaying 8x10 photos of babies allegedly father by Stank Stank. As he glared at the monitor, another older stagehand entered the waiting area with a wireless mic. Stank Stank turned around and bumped his head into the air. "Whut up Dawg?", he spoke. The stagehand attached the mic to the lapel of Stank Stank's blazer. He looked at the monitor and smirked, "Nice looking kids.", the stagehand announced.

"Daine Mine!", Stank Stank immediately informed. He looked the stage hand up and down. "You kinda old poddna, but om 'sho you know what a 'ho is. In case yo' mind slipping on ya', he pointed at the monitor,' dem 'ho's."

The stange hand walked out behind the curtain and whispered to Stank Stank, "Stand by in five, four, three, two.... "

"Ladies and Gentlemen, please welcome Marcell Robinson to the show!" The host called out.

Prepared to make his unforgettable television debut, Stank Stank flipped up the collar of his orange and white pinstripe blazer, put his hands in his pockets and proudly displayed his glistening dark chocolate chest as he strutted onto the stage.

While the studio audience booed and threw wodds of paper at him, he made hand gestures, gang signs and mouthed obscenities.

"Deadbeat!", a short stocky woman, from the front middle section, yelled.

"Fat Ass!", Stank Stank replied.

"Have a seat Mr. Robinson.", the host said to him. Stank Stank sat down in the vacant chair, crossed his legs and eyed all the women on stage as if he was viewing fine aged wine. As the camera focused on each lady, a split screen showed a photo of Stank Stank and the baby in question.

The host walked over to the first woman. "This is Shatonya', he said to the audience. 'Shatonya says, that one night she meet this young man', he pointed to Stank Stank, 'at a fast food place. The next week, he moved in with her. The week after that, he moved out. Eight and a half months later, she gave birth to a baby girl. Little Marshonna, who is now two years old, is here today to meet her daddy for the first time".

Stank Stank looked around the stage as if he was looking for another individual. "Yo Mane, you need to call dude on out hure, know what om sayn', Om jest hure fo my money yo".

"Uk um! Don't be frontin' like dat Mawcell!' , Shatonya yelled to him. 'You know dis baby yours. Gonna tell me you cain't have no babies 'cos you got hurt in service. I found out yo ass hadn't even not been in no service".

"Gurl, shat up!', Stank Stank shouted back,'dat what you get trying to dress all sexy and shit. What you expect? Dress like a 'ho, ya get treated like a 'ho, and dat baby ain't even not mine. You jist want somebody to give you some money. Dat's what you all want. Ain no fool. I know da 'sco".

"This is Dawnesha", the host said as he walked over to the next chair. Above her head the monitor showed a happy three year old playing with oversized rolling toys in the secluded baby-sitting area.

"Dawnesha says that she went to visit a friend on the Westside and ended up spending six weeks with Marcell Robinson!', he turned and points at Stank Stank. Nine months later, they became the proud parents of Donnicello." The audience watched as the baby boy giggled and cooed into the camera. Turning to look at the child, Stank Stank yelled out ,"What the hell kind of name is dat?! Soundin' like some kind of cautoon shit."

Dawnesha immediately jumped from her seat and ran over in front of Stank Stank.

"Why you worried 'bout his name? Huh? Why you cure. You say heen yours." Dawnesha screamed. The security guards rushed over and assisted the girl back to her seat and Stank Stank removed a cinnamon toothpick from his breast pocket and put it in his mouth.

"Om jest sayin' mane', he replied,' dat's fucked up'. He looked out into the audience and jumped out of his seat. "Oh snap!', he put his hand over his top lip, as if he was trying to cover his mouth,'lil dude kinda look like ole boy in the back row over thure!" He pointed out into the middle back section of the studio. "Hey mane, you not no pailsta or nuthin' aw ya, 'cuze I hur ya'll get all the women. Knowwhatimeant playa?" He asked. He started laughing wildly and sat back down just as the theme music begain to play.

After the commercial break, the host introduced Jakeena Jacobs and her young son, Marcel Robinson, Jr. Jakeena was tall for a young lady. An ex-track runner, she towered over five feet, nine inches. Her Large breast, fair complexion and long carefully weaved in artificial blond hair had always been an instant turn on for Stank Stank and he was doing all he could to keep from giving her his signature wink before whatever lame line he decided to use. He was still attracted to her, even though she had put on quite a bit of weight since the birth of the baby. He couldn't resist staring at her plump, red lips that he secretly remembered tasted like a warm rich creamy mocha latte that cold winter evening when the baby was conceived. Just like today, she was dressed for attention. Stank Stank had no problem imagining that day all over again. She was wearing a pair of skin- tight corduroy button fly jeans. As he sat there, preparing to deny paternity, he had the urge to flip a quarter into the cleavage of her form fitting sweater.

"Momma got it goin' on boy", he thought to himself as he rolled the toothpick around his lips, trying to ignore the happy little baby that was now smiling and cooing at him.

"Mane, I caint have no other junior, I got a junior back home dawg." Marcell acknowledged, rubbing the tangled up hair in the middle of his chest. His comment was ignored as the show continued.

Jakeena looked over at Stank Stank and gave him a disgusted smirk.

"I met Marcell at my friend, Chin Li Chu's Christmas party. I thought it was pretty strange, we both arriving two hours early that day. I felt like I overheard a different time or something. You know like Marcell suppose to have arrived at that time and I was suppose to arrive when everybody else did. You know what om sayin'?', she winked at the audience,' then ole girl was like ya'll come on in. Ya'll can go in my back room and look at a movie until I finish decoratin'. So, I was like okay, well maybe everything's okay. And so, me and Marcell, we went on in thur and then you know, it was this sad part and I started cryin' a little and Marcell was so sweet, he moved over closer to me and took dis soft lil o' handerchief from his pocket and wiped my tears and gave me a hug and stuff. From there, it was on like a pot of nake bones.", she said while squirving her neck.

"So you thought that your friend Chin Li Chu and Marcell here, were dating?", the host asked and looked at Stank Stank, while Jakeena nodded yes towards the audience.

"Mane, just cause Chin Li a cute, lil ole fine ass blackinknees you know the sustas gonna thank every mane out there gon wanna tap that.", Stank Stank replied.

"Excuse me', the host questioned,' I didn't quite get that. You called the friend what?" "Black-in-knees dawg', Stank Stank repeated,' you know, Black and Chinese. Mixed." He stood up and walked towards the end of the stage.

"But that's bull shit dare dough, ain been at no pordy", he lied. Jakeena jumped up almost tripping over her handbag. "Oh you lie!', she screamed,' you lie Marcell.

Stank Stank returned to his seat when Jakeena launched toward him with open hand. He was promptly saved from a vicious slap by set security.

"I wuzzn't at no pordy, not dat yure, I wuzzn't", he said.

"How old you think the baby is, Marcell", Jakeena asked.

"Hell girl, I'own know, he yo boy!" Stank Stank Shouted.

Just then the monitor showed the baby again as he was walking across the room to get a toy. The audience went quiet.

"Look at that walk!', Jakeena shouted, 'look at the shape of his face! Look at the tiny mole above his left eye and tell me that ain't his baby!"

"I wuzzn't at no poddy, not dat yure, I wuzzn't", he said.

"How old you think the baby is, Marcell", Jakeena asked.

"Hell girl, I'own know, he yo boy!" Stank Stank Shouted.

Just then the monitor showed the baby again as he was walking across the room to get a toy. The audience went quiet.

"Look at that walk!', Jakeena shouted, 'look at the shape of his face! at Look the tiny mole above his left eye and tell me that ain't his baby!"

Stank Stank leaned over towards the monitor and starred at the little toddler in shameful amazement. All eyes were on him as he scanned the baby from head to toe unable to deny the obvious fact that he was the father. Stank Stank, stood up, leaned forward, and pulled at his crotch.

"Oh my damn!, Shit! My bad mane. My bad,' he admitted,' dis one hure a maybe." He turned to Jakeena, "Damn gurl! I thought I seen you take the pill dat night!"

"I took an aspirin fool!', she yelled, 'my head was hurtin' from all the crying I was doing over dat movie."

"I got his twins!", the last girl yelled. The monitor switched to a set of three year olds. Stank Stank jumped up from his seat in an outrage.

"You aint got shit!', he hollered, wrinkling up his face as if he was in excruciating pain, 'dem babies white!", he announced, "Do I look like I got blue eyes? Omma black mane bitch!"

Almost immediately Jill begain sobbing.

"Dad said you wouldn't claim these babies Marcell', she swept.' I said he was wrong. I told everybody they were wrong." As the tears began to roll uncontrollably Stank Stank continued to deny the babies.

"Ain white dough!' he yelled. 'ain white, you b'line!, Ain white. That's some bullshit." With her voice shaking, Jill yelled out, "He was the only black man I was with that year and he told me every day, that we were together, that he loved me and that when he got a job, we were going to get married and raise our babies together. He knew when I got pregnant and he knew the babies were his. He even wanted me to name one of our sons Kobeon Labrontae Robinson."

"So what?!', Stank Stank asked,' I fed you a few lines. What dat suppose to do, automatically make me Willie Cornbread or somebody? You betta get the hell up outta hure. I 'sho aint payin' fo dem lil bastas!", he yelled.

Jill was so upset all she could do was run off stage, crying hysterically as the studio audience booed even louder at Stank Stank.

"Fuck ya'll!,' ya'll don't know shit! Nunna ya!"

Back home, just past eight o'clock in the morning, Mrs. Matty was rolling out of her old custom made bed with a velour headboard.

Yawning deeply, she stretched out her arms and dangled the flabs of fat as she worked out the night's stiffness. Slipping her feet into flowered leather house shoes, she grabbed the matching robe from the bottom of the bed and made her way down the hallway and into the dimly lit kitchen. She climbed upon the foot stool, retrieved a coffee cup from the cupboard and leaned over to lift the window shade, letting in the light of the mid-morning sun. She shuffled over to the table, sat down and poured herself a cup of coffee. When she turned on the portable 12" tv, the phone rang. With a dry throat, she took a quick sip of the warm coffee, allowing the phone to ring a second time, before answering

. "Good Morning", she said into the phone.

"Hey there, Lillie', she greeted, 'Stank Stank what?', she took another sip of coffee and added a spurt of honey to it. Say he is?, Where bought? What station, I mean", she asked. She took a left over biscuit from the breadbox and spreaded homemade peach perserves on it. "Mawcell Robinson, Stank Stank real name", she confirmed. "U Da Daddy", "Show 'nuff,' wait, wait, wait just a minute", she said while reaching over and turning the knob on the outdated television set.

"Well I'll be Lillie!', she shouted in excitement. 'Dat's him alright. Look at him sitting there all proud and handsome-fied. Um-hmm, don't he look nice? Damn fool ain't put no shut on though", she said in confusion.

"These young men thank dat look good Matty', Ms. Lillie told her, 'showing off they chest and thang to da girls. You know it ain't like it was when we were coming along. Yo private pods was yo private pods

"Uh-Hm", Mrs. Matty acknowledged her comment as she took another bite of the biscuit. "All dem babies heels, Matty?", Mrs. Lillie asked.

"Maybe', Mrs. Mattie answered. 'I knowed he 'spose to have right smart of

'em', she slurped the coffee and burped loudly. 'He got some out wes for sho, I hear. 'ran bout Annahine, and Sanna Bobba."

"Don't dey pay ya for being on dem shows Mattie?', Ms. Lillie asked,' cause he sho could use dat money. On 8'oclock news yessaday, dey say the po-east lookin' for dat boy. Something 'bout him not showing up in court."

Mrs. Mattie was busy watching the talk show. She broke off a chunk of tobacco and stuffed it into her cheek. Adjusting it with her tongue, she lined a paper cup with torn up pieces of paper. "Uhh-humm", Mrs. Mattie replied.

"Mattie', Ms. Lillie asked, 'Aint dat a white girl on the end, down by dat dough?"

"Ain know he had no white woman', Ms. Mattie admitted." Chewing steadily on her tobacco, she spat a flowing stream of thick brown liquid into the cup. As the residue dangled from her bottom lip, she reached over and got a paper towel from the holder and wiped her mouth.

"Coase, Stank Stank one of dem fellows who can have any woman he wants.', Mrs. Mattie told her, 'he's a real pretty boy when he clean up."

"Mattie, dem babies, there, don't look black. Dey got them funny color eyes and look at 'em. I thank dats a sham there", Ms. Lillie alerted.

As the theme music played and credits began to roll, the security guards rushed over and apprehended Stank Stank who was so heated that he was threatening to take on everyone in the studio and beat them to a bloody pulp.

"Just pay me my damn money!", he said as the guards walked him behind the curtians.

Once inside the stretch limo, Stank Stank removed his pinstripe blazer and two tone patent leather shoes. Immediately, he started pushing buttons and flipping switiches.

"Dis straight!", he approved. He flipped another switch and the back wall slid down revealing a two person hot tub as the fully stocked mini bar spun around in front of him. He pushed another button and the water in the hot tub started to bubble and warm.

"Yo Dawg!', he hollered, up front to the driver,'is dis a real hot tub mane?"

The light by the telephone lit up and Stank Stank reluctantly answered.

"Ah, hel-lo?", he waited curiously for a response.

"Yes sir, this is the driver.'

"No shit!, Damn Mane, you can even call me from the steering wheel?", Stank Stank interrupted.

"Yessir, well', the driver took a deep breath and continued,'if you need to speak with me, there's no need to yell, just pick up the phone. It'll buzz me."

"Aw-ight Mane, my bad", Stank Stank apologized.

The limo made a left turn onto a one way street and stopped at a red light. Stank Stank saw a tall slim lady wearing a mini skirt, high heels and a thin screen painted tee shirt. She was leaving a night club so he figured she'd be a easy pick up.

Besides, the high heels made her legs look long and silky smooth. Every step looked scrumptious to him as he watched her hips sway seductively from side to side. Unable to controll himself, he opened the moon roof and popped his head up.

"Hey baby!', he called to her,' you sho lookin' good tonight gurl." Shining a spot light towards his head, he flashed his gold, coffee stained teeth at her and extended his beefy tongue as far out of his mouth as he could and slowly ran it around his thick dry lips.

"You ever been wit a VIP sweet thang?", he asked. The young lady checked out his bare chest. Noticing his six pack, she slowed her steps and smiled at him.

Just as she began walking towards the limo, the light turned green and Stank Stank nearly gave himself a concussion trying to get back inside and stop the driver.

"Damn Mane!', he screamed in frustration,' you fuckin' up my game!", he yelled to the driver, whom he forgot could not hear him.

The telephone light lit up again and Stank Stank answered, nearly dropping the receiver as he smeared cocktail sauce all over the handset.

"Talk to me", he answered with a mouth full of boiled shrimp.

"Did you request something, Mr. Robinson?", the driver asked. Stank Stank swallowed the shrimp and took a few sips of sparkling water to clear his mouth.

"Mane, when we gone be at the hotel?', he asked, 'playa gettin' a little tied, ya know?" " We're pulling into the driveway right now sir", the chaffuer answered.

Stank Stank pulled a plastic bag from the inside of his blazer pocket and dumped the remainder of the boilered shrimp into it and closed the zipper.

"Deez comin' wit me", he said as he scanned the bar for other objects of interest. From the frig, he stuffed several mini bottles of alcoholic beverages into his pockets, along with two ashtrays and a cockscrew with the name of the limo company engraved on it. The chaffure stopped at the door of the hotel, got out of the limo, walked to the back and opened the door for Stank Stank.

"Hole up poddna, I can get my own dough', he advised,'ain no bitch ass nigga or nutthin'." "I apologize, Mr. Robinson', the chaffuer said,' standard procedure". He stepped back and placed his hands behind his back. "As you request sir."

"Damn right as I request', Stank Stank replied ,' omma VIP, up in dis junt.', he gave the chaffuer a brand new dollar bill that looked hot off the press,' and don't you forget it", he smiled.

Stank Stank crawled out of the limo with his blazer strategically rolled up in his arms to keep all of his treasures from falling out. It was cool inside the limo and his chest had gotten a little ashy. The small patch of tightly tangled chest hair above his six pack looked like a zillion little moles between his nipples.

He sported the orange and white pinstripe slacks half-way down his forrest green boxers that were now wedged in the upper middle of his backside. He spotted leftover cocktail sauce on his hand and fingers and quickly sucked it off before extending his hand to the chaffuer, who decided to give him a smile and nodd instead of a handshake.

"Time to call my ho's now', Stank Stank told him, ' brotha gotta get his freak on. KnowwhatImean playa?", He told the driver, as he strutted away from the car. Stank Stank entered the hotel room and scanned the area, letting the door slam shout behind him. The loud sound echoed down the hallway disturbing every guest on the floor. "Yeah, buddy', he said,' thad eels!" he went straight to the bed and retrieved a rich creamy chocolate mint from one of his pillows and stuck it in his mouth. Then, he kicked off his shoes and jumped onto the white satin sheets and rolled around on top of the bed, getting a kick out of the feel of the feather filled pillow top mattress.

"Oh Shit!", he shouted, realizing that one of the bottles of red wine had leaked onto the white satin comforter. He checked his blazer and found a huge red stain.

"Damn!', he cussed,' well, Ms. Mattie'll get dat out fa me", he thought.

He walked over to the Jacuzzi and turned the water on. Just then he saw a round button on the wall and several switiches nearby. He couldn't resist the temptation. He dashed over to the wall and started pushing buttons and flipping switches. He discovered a dimmer switch and a sound system. The sound system had been preloaded with love songs of the seventies and it gave him an idea. He pulled a mini bottle of whisky from his blazer pocket and gulped it down. Starting to get a change in attitude, he made his way to the bed where he decided to strip to his forrest green underwear and make a phone call.

"Hey baby, whatchu doing?", he smiled. The coffee and nicotine stains on his teeth were darkening. They looked as if he hadn't seen a tooth brush in five days.

"What you mean who dis is?" Dis Mawcell, Sweet thang, da luvo-fyalife. You gone and fugat 'bout me already? Baby thayne nice. What you got on gurl? You wearing dat cute little shawt robe wit da blue dragon on the back.?"

He looked over at the Jacuzzi and saw the water beginning to foam.

"Chow Li, look hure baby. Mawcell a lonely mane. Why don't you brang yo fine lil yellow ass on ova to dis hure hotel and let Mawcell putcha in dis Jacuzzi. Make you feel so good you'll thank you was back in Saigon or some damn whure?"

He rolled onto his back in the middle of the king size bed and slowly ran his hand over his stomach. "Dis jist a real nice room, and I got it fo you boo",he lied and begged. You know what I like 'bout you? You don't waste yo' time watching all dem talk shows and shit. You a real woman, baby. The kind that a mane like me need in his life fa evva!" He changed the tone of his voice."You know it's been a long time. Long time no see, know what I mean?', he paused briefly,' knoll dis ain't no booty call. Don't even trip like dat. " It became obvious that

Chow Li had seen the show and Marcell spent his last night in California alone.

The next day, Carson Perry International Airport was swarming with police cars. Every airplane that touched ground was invaded by highly professional security guards looking for Marcell Robinson. An arrest warrant was issued after the prosecuting attorney saw him on tv.

"We will be landing in approximately thirty minutes", the flight attendent announced over the loud speaker that awakened a sleeping Stank Stank, who was seated next to a guy flying into the United States on business. "We will be landing in approximately thirty minutes", the flight attendent repeated.

Stank Stank yawned and tried to stretch out his legs but the seat in front of him was too close. He sat up and wiped the drool from his mouth and flipped down the small overhead television. The message scrolling across the bottom of the screen told him that not only was he the newest VIP, but he was also wanted by police. He closed the tv compartment and quickly scanned the room. When he noticed that most of the people were busy with computers or sleeping, he grabbed his backpack, pretending to hold it out of the way, while partially covering his face. Quickly, he dashed towards the restroom. After relieving his bladder, he removed his red leather pants and replaced them with a pair of stained, ripped blue jeans. His expensive multicolor sneakers were replaced with a pair of plain black hightop basketball shoes that looked like he'd gotten them in the mid 1970s. He dawned a loose fitting faded out tee-shirt that read "Nuttin' but a playa". Adding to his disguise, he wore a fake moustache, a baseball cap, a sun visor, and a pair of round non prescription eye glasses. He returned to his seat leaving behind, an opened condom wrapper that fell out the pocket of his jeans. The guy seated near the aisle looked at him and smiled. "You know, that not work", he told Stank Stank while nodding quickly at his face. Stank Stank turned and looked at the stranger in disgust. "Hey mane, Omma VIP, okay, I gots to keep myself like dis", he told him.

"Mustache out there', the man replied, ' surely Americans won't go for it. It's too frizzy." Stank Stank looked at him and arched his eyebrow, "Yo ASS gonna be too frizzy if you don't shat the hell up!"

A flight attendant in a snug fitting uniform with large protruding breast walked by. Stank Stank starred at her constantly and tried to get her attention.

"Seep!", he whispered through his teeth, while eyeing the lady constantly. She totally ignored him. "Seep!, seep!", he repeated. When he realized that she appeared to be coming back his way, he tapped the guy in the aisle seat on the arm.

"Hey mane, switch seats wit me for a hot second," he told him.

The stranger smiled cheerfully,"Oh, no, I shat de hell up!', he said, 'mind business I do, American crazy", he smiled.

"Knoll mane, knoll, it ain't like dat", Stank Stank pleased. He took a twenty dollar bill from his pocket and handed it to the stranger.

"Oh thank you ', the stanger smiled and took the cash,' crazy American money worth much more in my country", he said while pretending to go back to sleep.

Not paying much attention to the stranger, Stank Stank was still in a standing position when a flat chested flight attendent walked over and asked him to sit down for landing. Stank Stank frowned at the stranger, who was watching him through one eye. "Hey mane,' Stank Stank said,' if you ain't gonna sit by the winda, you need to give me my money back."

"Seet by window', the stranger pretended to be asleep,' what's dis seet by window", he slurred, as the busty stewdess walked over and put a pillow behind his neck. She stroked his head and made sure his seatbelt was fastened. He smiled happily at her soft warm touch and fantasized in the midst of her sweet fragrant perfume.

"Heen sleep dough", Stank Stank disappointedly told the flight attendent.

Once on the ground, Stank Stank got off the airplane with no problem. While policemen and security guards swarmed the grounds looking for a flashy dressed, semi-cocky young man, Stank Stank strolled right pass them. He entered the airport walking swiftly with the backpack slung over his shoulder. His baseball cap was turned forward in the correct position and the clear, round shaped, non-prescription eyeglasses gave the appearance of a well- rounded college student returning home for a break. He followed the neon signs which led him to a room full of ancient looking payphones with one single automatic teller machine in the corner. There, he quickly deposited the bulk of his funds and hurried out front to hail a taxi.

A few minutes later, a staunted looking obese guy in a red and white four door vehicle squarved over to the curb.

"Taxi?", he yelled.

Without saying a word, Stank Stank opened the rear passenger door and climbed in. The driver, used to picking up celebrities from the airport, kept an eye on him as he raced through the parking lot, nearly missing pedestrians and parked vehicles along the way. Almost passing the entrance to the expressway, he made a sharp left turn onto Adams thoroughfare, throwing Stank Stank across the back seat. Stank Stank, once settled, begin transitioning back to himself. He'd just removed the baseball cap and eyeglasses when the driver slammed the brakes just inches from a stalled truck with flashing hazard lights.

Pausing, the cabby pulled down his visor and looked candidly at Stank Stank, who had been thrown into the plastic partision that separted the back seat from the front.

"You, I knew it!', the cabby smiled excitedly, 'Mr. Big Shit Popping back in town!"

Stank Stank glanced at him, still slightly upset from being slammed into the plexi-glass but, loving the sudden fame at the same time, wasn't sure how to respond.

"Need to watch the skreet mane", he told him. "So what you do 'bout all dem bitches after you bro'?", the cabby asked. Backing up suddenly, he slammed the car into first gear, then third and almost accidentally jumped the meridian trying to go around the stalled truck.

"I know what Ida told 'em', he continued,' Ida told 'em go straight to hell 'ho;

Get yo' child support there!"

Stank Stank was finally out of disguise, but tried to play things off since he was a wanted man who had just been identified by a man with a CB radio.

"You got me confused dawg", he replied calmly. The driver shifted back into third gear and then fifth and gently hit the bumper of another cabby.

"Mane Shit!", Stank Stank yelled, starting to lose his cool.

"Aw-we straight', the cabby assured him,'that's my girl. Gotta let the shawteez know we on dey ass, watchin' shit. Ya feel me playa?", he asked trying to talk like the local thugs.

"What you said, Stank Stank agreed as he puffed on a menthol cigarette. He was starting to feel the fame. He was back home and V I P status was in the air. "So where you goin', the cabby asked,' just the North Side?" He slammed the brakes again and turned suddenly onto the off ramp. Stank Stank dropped the cigerette in his lap and swiftly leaped upward. "Yo tip on the line dawg!", he warned getting more and more upset. The cabby, not liking Stank Stank's comment, tried to justify his actions. "Oh, so what, you rather I have an accident rather than prevent one? Cut me some slack man", he said.

Stank Stank had had enough. "Look Mane', he said, ' jist let me out across the bridge; second red light near Ninety-Eight and Bufferscone."

The cabby still upset at Stank Stank's remark, picked up speed and started aggressively darting in and out of traffic, passing other vehicles with only inches to spare. Stank Stank held on silently, and waited. The cabby crossed the bridge and drove slowly towards the first red light. Thinking that Stank Stank wasn't paying attention, he quickly flicked the milage meter with his right hand. Stank Stank watched through partially closed eyes as the meter jumped up an additional fifty dollars. When the cabby was about to stop at the second light, Stank Stank saw a police car heading in their direction and decided to bale on the bill. He leaped from the backseat just as the the second red light turned red. He hurried down the side ally, leaped over a wooden fence and ran about a half block farther before stopping to catch his breathe. In the distance he could hear the police car pulling over the cabby who ran a red light in an attempt to chase him down for payment.

"Damn Right!', he yelled,' you don't know me like dat! Omma V I P bra' mane. Betta reckonize!"

He stepped around the corner and walked down the side walk. Although he was only two blocks from his studio apartment, he decided to stop at Flabby's for a bite to eat. Flabby's was dimly lit. The entire room seemed to move as the thick smoke floated in the air. Through the smoke, you could smell the stench of burnt chicken wings and stale beer. Stank Stank was scanning the room looking for a corner booth near the back of the room, when he heard a shout out. He stood still and tried to focus and listen for the voice again.

"Cell!", the voice shouted once more. Stank Stank walked towards the back of the room and saw a white napkin waving in the air.

"Ova hure poddna!", the voice directed. As Stank Stank slowly moved towards the voice, he realized that it was his homeboy Easyslide.

"Damn Mane', Stank Stank told him,'smile or sumptin' shit. It's dawk in hure, cain't nobaddy see yo' ass."

"Sit yo' poplar VIP ass down", Easyslide told him smiling.

Admiring the sight of freshly prepared hot wings on the table, Stank Stank walked closer to the booth The smell along made his stomach growl. Easyslide picked up a wingette and dipped it into some tan colored sauce and took a bite. Putting the meat down, he licked his fingertips and grabbed a napkin to remove dried sauce from his chin. Stank Stank slid into the booth across the table from him and looked out at the crowd hoping to see a waitress walking by.

"Dig in!', Easyslide told him, 'dis on me since you a big time VIP and shit." He took another bite of the wingette, taking and grissle and all into his mouth as

He chewed down on the end of the bone. He looked out at a petite waitress dressed in a mini skirt and braless tank top. While still eyeing the waitress, he picked up a extra large mug of light beer and took a huge gulp. The glass almost slipped through his greasy fingers as he turned his head to the side and let out a monstrous burp.

"I need to get with dat.", he told Stank Stank.

Stank Stank was holding a wingette and looking anxiously around the room.

"Mane where da hot sauce at?", he asked seriously.

"Thad eels", Easyslide told him, pointing towards the napking holder. Easyslide turned towards the bartender while stuffing his unswallowed food into one side of his cheeks.

"Spawn!, tell Flabby to get me another twelve homie, and add some jojos wit 'em". He turned back to Stank Stank, " Om so hungry. I went by momma's and all she had was a lil bitty bowl of left over peas and hog mawgs. Playa can't roll like dat, knowwhatomsayin? I gots to eat."

Stank Stank picked up another piece of meat and doushed it with hot sauce,

"Fo Sho!", he agreed.

Easyslide dipped another mini drumstick into the sauce and placed it in his mouth. He wiggled his face around for a few seconds and pulled out a meatless bone. He then took a jojo from the platter and squarted a blob of ketchup on it, opened his mouth, displaying a lump of chewed food, and stuffed the pototoe wedge inside. A clump of ketchup oozed from the corner of his mouth as he attempted to talk to Stank Stank.

"Whatja say 'bout it?', he asked while swallowing the half-chewed food. He picked up the beer mug and slurped in half the liquid. Stank Stank licked leftover hot sauce off his fingertips and grabbed a potato wedge.

"Bout what?", he asked, after clearing his mouth.

Easyslide wiped his hands on some used napkins that he had by his plate and eyed Stank Stank inquistedly.

"All dem 'lil fuckas you got?", he asked, giving Stank Stank his serious wide eyes.

"I'own even not know', Stank Stank answered. 'One might be mine. Test can be wrong dough." Just then, the waitress returned to the dinning area and Easyslide made eye contact with her and winked.

"Omma hit dat!', he shared with Stank Stank,' see how she lookin' at me, like she all suditty and shit? Dem da mane ones be wontin' it."

He rubbed his greasy, chicken smelling hands on his jeans, got up and approached the waitress. At five feet, five inches tall and one hundred fourty-seven pounds, his small frame made him hard to see in the crowd. He slid behind the waitress and pinched her on the left leg, just below the hem of her hot pants. Out of surprise, she turned around instantly. He glared at her name tag and smiled, showing several missing teeth.

"Hey La-Keisha', he said pointing at her name tag, 'how 'bout me and you go on a picnic tomorrow over in the pogg? We can get us some 'lil meat rolls in a can, some crackas and some scrawbarries. Hell girl, after all dat, we may need a blanket. Don't let my small appearance fool ya.', he smiled flirtingly and grabbed his crotch,' you only seein' da small podds now." He laughed wildly and slapped her on the backside.

LaKeisha, who stood about six inches higher than Easyslide, looked down at him and fluttered her eyes in confusion.

"I know you didn't just slap my ass Easyslide", she said. All of a sudden, everything seemed to go instantly into slow motion, as her head popped back and her neck started to wiggle and turn, in every possible position imaginable and unimaginable.

"AIN GOT NO TIME FA A WONNA BE PLAYA LIKE YOU!', she told him,'I NEED ME A STABLE MAN. SOMEONE WIT A GOOD STEADY JOB WHO CAN HELP ME TAKE CURE MY KIDZ, SO DON'T BE COMMIN' OVER HURE TRYIN' TO ACT ALL MIGHTY JOE HUNG , GRABBING ON YO SHIT!." She started to walk away, but turned around, " OH, AND SLAP ME AGAIN, OMMA CUT YO' ASS!"

Slightly embarrassed, Easyslide moved back to his booth and stood against the wall trying to inconspicuously dig out a wedgie that was starting to hurt him worse than the awful taste of rejection. After releasing his underwear, he looked at Stank Stank and tried to muster up a smile. He grabbed his waist band and pulled up on the front of his jeans.

"Bitch know she wont somma dis." he assured himself as he sat down.

CHAPTER SIX

The Retaliation

Across town, at the hospital, Spicey was resting in the comfortable cushioned hospital bed counting down days to be released. Just after lunch, she got a visit from a good friend. Ocean Breeze walked in wearing skin tight, pink leather pants and a turquiose knit sweater. His large open toe sandles displayed perfectly painted toe nails in the same color as his sweater. His permed auburn hair hung just below his shoulders and his breast set up high and perky.

"Wake up honey, I need you to take a look at my wax job.', he said to Spicey who was starting to nodd off, 'I have to go on stage tomorrow and I don't need a man beard showing." He glided straight to the mirror and checked his face for a five o'clock shadow. "Oh, I do suppose that if anything appears, I can always cover it with more make up", he added.

Spicey sat up and smiled when she saw Ocean Breeze. Somehow, no matter how bad things were, Ocean Breeze had a way of making it better. He walked over to the side of the bed, reached into his clevage and pulled out a thick rubber breast cup. "Look! I got new boobies!", he announced. Spicey smiled approvingly.

"I thought you was going to get yo' own.", Spicey reminded him.

"I did', Ocean stated,' I paid for them, 'so they're mine", he smiled. He re-positioned the padding into the sweater and sat on the bed.

"I need more money for the real thing dearie", he told her.

Spicey struggled slightly and set up higher in the bed. She held her right side and leaned towards Ocean. "I wanna get that bastard real good.", she confessed.

Ocean Breeze looked at Spicey and waved a pointed finger across her face.

"He's not worth going to jail for honey', he told her,' you have to learn to expect certain things doing what we do."

Spicey moved away from Ocean and an angry look came across her face.

"Ain letting' it go!', she said harshly,' it's not like he only kept my money. You and the whole world heard about how they found me. I want to humiliate him just like that!"

Ocean looked at her, wrinkled his forehead, and sighted heavily before reaching out and giving her a tight hug.

"We'll get him, but give me time', he told her,'I have to notify my posse. After you are released, you will come stay with me for a while until you heal better. During that time, we will plan everything perfectly. I know people who will change his life."

Mrs. Matty was sitting on the front porch in a wooden rocking chair watching the neighborhood activities when Lilly rode up on her motorized scooter.

Mrs. Matty, who had been rocking and chewing, picked up a small foam cup next to her chair and deposited an ounce of dark fluid from her mouth. She looked at Lilly and giggled.

"Omma get me one of dem thangs one of deez days,'she said,' come on up here Lilly." Mrs. Lilly smiled and drove the scooter up the ramp and onto the front porch next to Mrs. Matty.

"You can sit in datchaire, you wont", Mrs. Matty told her, while pointing to an old rusty yard chair next to the door.

"Ain getting' up ', Mrs. Lilly told her,' this seat comfortable." She backed the scooter next to Mrs. Matty and parked.

"I just came by to see if you hud 'bout that juvenille case over in Gwenavere. They got this one 'lil girl in custody, mind me so much of Stank Stank sister. Grad goodness!', she said, 'made me wonder if that girl ever had a baby".

"Hell yeah, she had some babies!,' Mrs. Matty confessed, 'she been so busy ho'n, sheen had no time to raise nam one. Tell me, she done way wit two or three", she paused and picked up her cup to deposited more liquid before continuing, ' gave two, I thank, to the state."

Mrs. Lilly picked up a geriatric style protein drink and took a sip.

"Well, Ain gossiping Matty,' she said, ' but I hud she had one when she was just a girl haself; hud it s'pose to b'loan to some boy dey call Easyslide. Say he and dat girl used to stay 'round each chudda and thangs."

"James Teller?', Mrs. Matty asked out of surprise. 'noll see, dey did stay 'round each chudda, but dat's 'cause ha daddy and J. T's aint tee was shackin' up back then. Dayne his baby dough cause she was smellin' after some new boy ya call Reno. He was from outta town somewhere; thank his folks had a lil money or sumpt'n. He was just sixteen and had a lil bitty sports ca. He always was takin' ha to da picture show and buying her 'pensive nacklaces and perfumes and thangs. When he told his folks dat his girlfriend, who was fo years up under his age, was pregnutt, they went and ship him off to service school. Dat 'ho didn't even know the boys full name so she gave the baby ha last name. But yeah, dat's da daddy. Reno. Um hum", she said as she split the clump of chew into the cup."

Mrs. Matty leaned back and took a deep breath. "I wonda when she getting' out da hospital. I know the motel been losing money since she been laid up hut and all". "Matty, I caint place dis Reno boy", Mrs. Lillie said, rubbing her forehead. One of the neighborhood kids ran by, otopped, picked up a weekly newspaper from the driveway and threw it upon the porch, barely missing her spit cup.

"Thank ya baby!', Mrs. Matty yelled out,' Damn boy almost knocked my cup over." she mummered to Lillie as she pushed the cup closer to the wall.

"Reno was dat 'lil square head boy. Look did like a squll in da face. He was tall, skinny and light skindid wit dem funny colored eyes. He always wo matching clothes, wit his shut tucked in, and kept his head shaved low and neat. He like did dat crazy white boy music. You know, that loud, screaming rock and roll", Mrs. Matty explained.

"Did his folks move into dat two story house 'round on Adrian Cove?", Mrs. Lillie asked.

"Um-hum, uh-hum, show did', Mrs. Matty told her smiling and nodding her head. "I r'memba dat 'lil squll face boy!" Mrs. Lillie said excitedly.

Just outside of China Town, Ocean Breeze parked the two door hatchback in the driveway and took off his high heel shoes and reached in the back seat to get Spicey's bags. He walked briskly around to the passenger side of the car and helped Spicey onto her feet. "Put your weight on me honey', he told her,' I'm stronger than I look." Putting a protective arm around her waist, he lead her to the door of his apartment. "Now hang onto the wall here, while I get the door open. All you have to do is make it to the couch and you'll be comfortable there for a while", he told her.

He opened the door and revealed quadrupple colored custom made carpeting that looked like a well overgrown spray painted lawn. A thick plastic strip ran from the door to an open closet where he kept various types of shoes along with a small box and new terry cloth house shoes.

"Here Hon', Ocean instructed,'kick your shoes off in the closet. I don't allow them on my carpet." Spicey carefully slipped her feet out of her shoes and continued to the living room. Each wall was painted a different color just like the carpeting. Spicey paused to take in the sight.

"Let me give you a quick show around the room", Ocean said noticing Spicey's expression. He walked a little farther into the wide open living room.

"The colors coincide with how I feel at certain times. The purple wall, with it's lilac carpeting represents a mellow, relaxed me', he said while placing a hand on his hip.' The pink wall, with the hot pink carpeting, represents my feminine side.

I sit in this area when I'm feeling more lady-like." He winked at Spicey who arched an eyebrow. This baby blue wall with it's medium blue carpeting represent an mellow me. Then here's my grey wall with the medium grey carpeting. This is my uncertainty area, where I sit and drink red wine and try and figure out my life".

He helped Spicey over to the couch, which was in the blue area.

"Oh, this is good', Ocean commented as Spicey sat on the couch,' the mellow section can help you chill out." He hurried down the hallway to get a blanket and pillow. "Lay down. Try and get comfortable! I'll be right back", he yelled from the hallway.

Almost instantly, he returned to the living room and located Spicey's medicine bag. Hurrying into the kitchen, he got a bottle of water and put the two tablets into spicey's mouth. "You should try and get some rest. I have a few friends coming over later for a round or two of poker', he told her,' after everything get going, we'll discuss things." He kissed her cheek and laid the blanket on top of her.

Spicey awakened later that evening thinking that she had been swept into dreamland. Just opening her eyes seemed like she was seeing everything for the first time. The entire apartment appeared to be under a huge black light. On the grey wall, the carnival poster, with the empty carousel, now showed tiny nude men with big muscles sitting on horses and leaning against thin black poles and there were naked fairies floating in the air over the Ferris wheel. She hadn't seen that when she walked in. As she turned her head to focus on the other new sights, her senses picked up the smell of lavender coming from a single stick of burning incense placed over an ashtray near the purple wall. Thinking she awakened somehow in the midst of a dream, she closed her eyes and returned her head to the pillow. Ocean Breeze sat at the wooden card table, in the middle of the kitchen, with three other drag queens. On Wednesdays, they'd get together for a friendly game of poker, have a few beers and discuss local gossip. In short, they had become accustomed to a weekly bitch session. Each one, having been born male in gender, loved the taste of an expensive flavored cigar along with ice cold beer. Ocean's posse included Jassy Teardrop, a medium framed muscular dancer with an explosive temper and a domastic violence rap sheet longer than Florida's panhandle. He started using the last name Teardrop after he was repeatedly found crying in a closet after several attacks on various partners. To remind him of his temper, he had a pink teardrop tatooed just above his right cheek.

Treasury Chest was closer to the real thing than any of them. He had actual breast and a clevage. He loved dressing sexy in thin low cut shirts and blouses. With his long bleached blond hair and naturally hazel eyes, he was considered extremely skilled in the art of seduction.

Querry was a perky twenty-one year old, fresh out of the closet. With his tanned skin and baby-face appearance, he was one of the top request at the playhouse. He and Ocean became friends a few months ago when he was looking for work. Ocean, being nearly twice his age, became an instant role model to him.

Ocean leaned back in the chair and sloughed down. The top of his black multi-striped robe fell open to his waist, revealing red silk boxers with black lace. With the cigar dangling from the corner of his mouth, he gazed intensely at the cards in his hand.

"I fold.", he said wearily, discarding the cards onto the table. He poured a shot of whiskey and slammed it down his throat. It was poker night and if he got bent, so be it. It was their day to be themselves and he had to come up with a way to help Spicey and keep everyone, especially Querry, out of jail at the same time. He didn't quite know how to bring up the subject.

"Let's take a break', Jassy suggested,' I have a wicked piss that doing a hell of a job on my bladder." He left the table and hurried off to the bathroom.

Querry finally finished a can of beer that he'd been drinking for thirty minutes or more and looked inquistedly at Ocean.

"What's wrong Cool Breeze?', he asked,' you seem to have something on your mind." He poked out his pouty lips and picked up a potatoe chip with two fingers and placed it ever so carefully into his mouth.

"Just gathering thoughts love. Give me a moment." Ocean replied in his regular man voice. Treasury looked over at Querry and winked." Maybe we're the only lucky ones today." Hmm', Querry responded, 'Louis and Clarke was fun!"

"You don't say', Treasury said,' I still can't believe the exploration."

"O! Kayyyy!", Querry responded arching his brows. He picked up a napkin and gently dabbed the corners of his mouth. Jassy returned to the table.

"That was harsh." He shared, while grabbing more beer from the frig.

Seeing the cards scathered on the table, Jassy gathered them up.

"Are we still playing or what?," he asked.

Ocean slurped down the remaining ounces of beer. After an invigorating burp, he leaned forward and re-lit the cigar. Hesistating, he poured another shot of whiskey and slammed it.

"Any of you know Wang Li Chu?", he blurted. All went quiet as several layers of tension filled the air. Jassy reached for the whiskey bottle and drank it down like water for nearly 10 seconds, before carefully sliding it over to Querry and lighting a cigerette. Querry refused to make eye contact with anyone. Instead, he kept his head down and waited.

"I think we all know the bastard.", Treasury said.

"I'm just waiting for a chance to kick his obnoxious ass", Jassy commented.

Seeing the sudden distant look on Querry's face, Treasury leaned over and stroked his head. "What did he do to you, honey?", he asked.

"I have an older sister, Quetina', he said, ' when I was eighteen, she was in college. She rented a small cottage off campus and I moved in with her to get away from the folks. One weekend, she went to a party and met this guy. She really liked him. He had money, a nice car, and lived in a wealthy neighborhood. After going out meeting him a few times, she decided to let him come over to the house and pick her up. The first time he saw me, he gave me a cold dark stare. When Quetina came into the room, she kissed my cheek and said she'd be home later. When they made it to the car, he opened the door for her, she got in.

He came back in the house to get his sunglasses. He grabbed them off the coffee table and yelled out to me.....

" Hey boy! There's a cute little girl next door, about your age. Why are you in here? Waiting for her brother to drop by?" I didn't respond to him because only my sister knew my preference. I didn't even look at him. I just kept watching tv., so he continued. "Hey!, Hey boy! You do know you're a boy right? I'm talking to you, boy! Maybe you want this. You want this, don't you? ' He grabbed his crotch. I knew it!' He slapped me on the back on the head and shouted, "Grow one boy!"

Something happened at the party and they came back early. I was in my boxers watching a movie with my date. A sad scene came on and I leaned over to comfort him. Next thing I knew, I was being yanked off the couch by the waistband of my Boxers. He held me with one hand, while he struggled to get his thick leather belt off with the other. I tried to fight him off, but it's hard to do when you got a razor sharp wedgie. I was wiggling terribly and trying to break free, but I couldn't, he was too strong. He pushed me against the wall and snatched off my boxers. He tossed me nude across the room. I fell onto the wood floor and he rushed over and started beating me unmercifully with the thick belt. My sister was frantic and screaming hysterically. Finally, she calmed down enough to call the police. By the time they got there, he was gone", he recalled. Querry put his head in his hands and cried silently.

"He made everything so hard', he wept,' so, so hard."

Treasury stroked Querry's back and inhaled a can of beer. Covering his mouth, he burped softly.

"His homophobic ass once pushed me out the back seat of a limo on Henton Highway in the middle of the night,' Treasury shared,' I almost got run over by an eighteen wheeler, but I got up in time and was knocked into the emergency lane by a compact hatchback."

Ocean stretched and yawned. Farting, he coughed and burped again. "Pardon me', he said, ' Where are my manners? Why did he push you out sweetie, what happened?" "I'd just finished performing one Saturday, it was early morning, around 3:30. Normally, I'd take off my dress or change into a pair of old blue jeans and sneakers for a quick walk home. That night I was exhausted. A storm was in the forecast and I could hear the thunder moving in, so I skipped changing clothes, put my sneakers on, grabbed my unbrella and headed home. I was a block and a half away from my loft when this shiny white stretch limo pulled up next to me, just as the rain began to fall. " Hey there pretty lady', he said,' can a nice gentleman offer you a ride?"

At first, I said no because I wanted to go straight home and get into a nice hot bubble bath, but he was persistent. When he offered to take me somewhere for a quick tasty drink and chat, I accepted, like an idiot, and got into the car. From the mini bar inside the limo, under the moon roof, he mixed up a couple apple martini's and we drank them, under the moonlight, with our arms intertwined. He smelled of freshly cut dollar bills as he leaned in and planted a soft kiss on my lips. Then he said that we needed to stop by his house so that he could pick up his wallet. Telling the driver to take the scenic route, he pointed towards Henton

Highway. He lowered the volume on the back radio and dimmed the lights, his hands started to wonder. What can I say? When he found the steak instead of the taco, he burst my lip, gave me a black eye and kicked me out the door into traffic." "He owes me four hundred dollars for teaching him how to do The Royal Shindig, on short notice, for some ball he was going to last year. I had to cancell six lessons I had scheduled that day. When it was time for him to pay up, he said he'd send someone over. Yeah, he sent someone over all right. Two hours later, he sent two thugs over to trash my studio and throw cupcakes at me. When they were done nearly destroying my studio, the big one growled , " Li Chu said Thanks". I tried calling Chu afterwards, but he changed his phone number," Jassy said looking aggrevated. The kitchen grew deadly quiet. They knew it was time to do what they felt in their hearts, was needed to be done. Ocean stood up and poured everyone a final shot of Burnt Water Whiskey. As it sat in the shot glasses before them, she asked for their help in conquring Wang Li Chu.

"That young lady healing on my couch in there is his latest victim. She's a good friend of mine. You may have heard about her on the evening news', Ocean said,' she is the one and only Spicey Robinson."

Familiar with the story, all eyes fell silently upon Spicey, who was unaware at the time, of what was happening.

Treasury leaped from the chair and banged his fist onto the table.

"Group meeting at the theatre next week!', he yelled,' we're going to need the little people!" They toasted in unison," To retaliation".

Clara Matty, have ya hud?!', Ms. Lilly yelled excitely into the telephone,' I knowed it was gonna happen. I just knowed it!"

"What you know Lilly, that got you all high up", Mrs. Matty asked her. Ms. Lilly took a deep breath and proceeded.

"Out in Chinatown, where dat ho Spicey likes to hang 'round, there dis fella namma Wang Li Chu. Tell me some lil bitty mane broke in his house and was robbin. He came home and saw em wit a sod slang across his back, so Li Chu grabbed his sod and dey stodded fightin'.

"Whatchu sey!" Mrs. Matty responded

"Yeah girl', Lilly continued, 'they got a fightin', the lil mane slid twinx his laids , and sliced him open pretty good down younder".

"Say heel woman now?, heh, heh, heh,." Mrs. Mattie teased.

"Midas Websta be." Mrs. Lilly giggled.

Mrs. Matty leaned back in her ole olive green chair and started turning the dial on the ancient television set.

"Da mane kilt im?", Matty asked.

" Knoll, his daudda, Chow Li was in town to see a friend and she had stopped by to see im. She found im in da house trembling' in a pool of blood and she call fa help.

"Dessa shame". Mrs. Matty said..

"It was on that Chinatown Radio news show dis morning' Matty", Mrs. Lillie told her. "What his dodda name again?", Mrs. Matty's asked.

"Chow Li". Lilly responded.

"Dat gull was in town to see Stank Stank, I betcha dat', Mrs. Matty informed while searching for the local news. 'I bleave he was messin' round wit a China gale at one point".

The same day, One hundred twenty-five miles away in Myron County, being put into the back of a squad car was a rambunctious preteen with a sassy mouth, big ideas and a taste for quick money.

"You need to calm down!", the officer yelled as placed the handcuffs around her wrist. " And you need to get yo stank breath out my face!", the little girl yelled back, still wiggling uncontrollably. "You're under arrest young lady", the officer told her while gently pushing her into the back seat of the car and slamming the door.

"No Shit!', she told him,' do I look like I think we're about to party up in here?", she asked sarcastically. She laid on the back seat and kicked at the window to get the officer's attention. "You can't keep me!', she screamed,' I ain't spray no words on no wall. I'm a minor! You'll get in big trouble!"

The ride to the police station didn't seem to frighten the child at all. In fact, she looked at it as popularity points. She didn't think about how it would make her mom feel, or what her dad would think about the situation. The only thing she cared about was how to tripple her allowance and get the things she wanted.

"Get out!', the policeman commanded as he opened the door,' you're going into holding until we can contact your parents."

"My mama don't get home until five o'clock", she said.

"What about your daddy?' the other officer asked,' or are you one of those daddy's babies."

"Man fuck you!', she replied,' I got a daddy. He a truck driver and won't be back until next week." The officer opened the door to the large steel cage, pushed the little girl inside, and slammed the door.

"Turn around so I can get the cuffs", he told her. Just then a female officer came around the corner with a tall skinny lady wearing a white mini skirt and a beige halter top. She had on a heavy application of make up, no shoes and her weave was missing in sections. She looked like she had ran right out of her shoes through some kind of dirt field.

"So what's your name, kid?', the cop asked as he removed the handcuffs.

The little girl looked worriedly at the new lady as the female cop pushed her into the same cell.

"People call me Angel Face", she answered while looking curiously at the tall skinny lady who was sharing her cell.

"You think you're living up to that nick name", he asked.

"Ain't do nothing man!', she yelled, while stomping over to sit on the hard cold bench. As the officer left the area, the new lady looked at the little girl and smirked. Angel Face starred at her. The weird looking lady sat on the other end of the bench, leaned against the wall and blew a huge bubble and popped it loudly. After giving her a long once over, Angel Face decided it was okay to communicate.

"You got some mo gum', she asked,' I sure could use a piece since I don't', she paused,' since ain got no mo smokes", she said, trying to sound tough. She walked over to the cell door, grabbed two bars and shook them.

"Fuckin' cops!', she called out,' I'll tell you what you can do. She leaned over, pulled her dress up and dropped her panties right in front of the cell camera.'arrest this!", she told them. She had no idea that she was under survaillance inside the cell. The hooker giggled, showing several missing front teeth. She leaned over and tossed the little girl a individually wrapped piece of brightly colored ball of bubble gum.

"I thank dey already arrested dat, but nice try," she told her. Angel Face unwrapped the bubble gum and put it in her mouth. She looked at the hooker again and noticed that she wasn't wearing a bra.

"My mama bought me a bra', she told the hooker,' mama said when a young lady get enough to show nipples through a shirt, it's time for a one." Getting hungry, Angel Face looked down at her twenty-four caret gold and pewter cartoon character watch. "My mama commin' to get me", she told the hooker. She walked over to the cell door and listened briefly to the conversation around the corner, and walked back over to question the prostitute.

"How come you ain't got no shoes on?" the little girl asked as she attempted to blow a large bubble.

"The pigs took'em', she told the child,' what are you anyway, some little private school prep kid? What's with the little plaid dress and thin knee high socks? What you do, steal somebody's lunch money and dey brought you here tryin' a scare ya straight?", the hooker questioned.

"Like I told them pigs', she said , trying to use the hooker's term,' I plead the filth?" "Angel Face', the lady cop yelled out.'get your butt over here and give me your name, address and phone number."

Angel Face wanted to mouth off to her, but she'd seen how she slammed the hooker up against the wall and yanked on her hair. That alone made her want to cooperate.

"Angel Face', she told the officer,' 77 David Anthony Court. It's a trailer park and we aint got no phone. "The officer snatched her up by the coller of her shirt and starred blankly into her eyes.

"Look litte girl. I have worked 24 hours steight, Im tired as hell, and I go home in thirty minutes and start enjoying my seven days off. Now you can either give me your real name or stay locked up in jail with Juicy the hooker for the next seven days. Im telling you now, I don't give a shit!", she snarled, while lifting the child off the floor.

"My name is Darvenity Jones Maam", she said in a shakey voice. As the tears began to build up in her eyes, she added," we aint got no phone, ' somebody gotta go get my momma." The officer signed heavily and pushed her away.

Darvenity's mother arrived within minutes after receiving a visit from the school principal about how the child was hauled off in a squad car for vandalism.

She rushed to the child's side. "Whatever you did we will discuss it at home", she told her,' I have to get to work".

The lady looked suspiciously at Juicey who sat there licking what looked like left over powder residue from the inside of her elbow. She had deep dark circles around her blood shot eyes. Her pink hair flowed raggedly over her thin crop top, exposing her very thin deep dark body. She looked at Darvenity's mother and smiled widely, exposing a mixture of missing and rotten teeth.. "Hi you?', she asked, while moving closer to the cell door,' you stay in a trayla pogg. You know where I can get some dust?" Pulling the child away from within reach of the strange lady still behind bars, she asked the her inquizzedly, "Who's your friend?" Darvenity looked at her mother with wide eyed innocence and responded, "That's Juicey momma. She a crack head 'ho."

* * *

ABOUT THE AUTHOR

Sybil Darlette grew up in the suburbs of the mid south, and was teased daily, as a child, for using proper English. For her, holding down various jobs offered a closer look and study into urban life and sociology. Soon, she decided to listen a bit closer to how things were being said around her. She found it amusing as well as educational. What if others could read what she was hearing? With much thought and consideration, she decided to put what she heard on paper and create amusing works of urban fiction. She currently resides in Ohio.

www.ingramcontent.com/pod-product-compliance
Lightning Source LLC
Chambersburg PA
CBHW072012170626
46813CB00005B/2121